# Animal Colony

*A cautionary tale
for today*

Thomas Allen Rexroth
&
Mark Andrew Olsen

Thomas A. Rexroth & Mark Andrew Olsen

Copies available at

# Dedication

This book is dedicated to all our children and grandchildren. May they have the same or better opportunities to have a happy and prosperous life than we did. May we pass on to them a country worthy of sacrifice.

# Prologue

Would the Animals choose to return to slavery, only this time a slavery of their own making?

Or would they choose to return to the uncertainty of freedom?

Perhaps we can find out by starting at the beginning.

The night of their escape…

Thomas A. Rexroth & Mark Andrew Olsen

# Chapter One

The Animals' flight to freedom began on the fourth day of a fateful November, when a bitter wind swept out of the north to scour the walls of the continent's lone British settlement.

With its arrival blew not only a blanket of arctic fog, but chilling threats of a harsh winter to come. Chasing out the lingering daylight, an icy mist drifted over from the nearby river and filled the fort's deserted courtyard.

Suddenly, a wooden clatter echoed across the void. It was the sound of someone slamming a cabin's window shutter against the cold.

The noise rang out again.

Then a third time.

In the dimming stalls of the palisade's Animal shelter, Hoss, a powerful workhorse twelve years of age, pricked up his ears at the racket. He blinked knowingly at his nearby friend, a respected goose named Gander.

The pair eyed each other with somber expressions.

Hoss dreaded the sound, for he knew right away what it meant. Its cruel echo filled his mind with the despair of endless nights, frosty mornings and a gnawing sense of having been forgotten by the world.

It was the sound of being left out in the cold.

There was no doubt: the closing of shutters meant their Masters were retreating indoors for the season. In the past, this ritual meant that until spring, humans would appear only now and then to toss the occasional bundle of hay or cupful of grain down into the feeding trough. This fall, however, their feedings had gone from meager and infrequent to almost none at all.

Hoss was a wise and perceptive horse, and his years as a barnyard leader had taught him how to read the signs of a difficult winter. Every sign he knew told him they were in for a brutal period. He had noticed warnings like his own, unusually shaggy coat, and the sows' insistence on lining their nests with twigs and pine needles, the larger-than-normal squirrels' nests, even the cows' restlessness in their pens. All of these told Hoss they were in for a brutal time.

His only consistent signs of human life would be plumes of greasy smoke billowing from the cabins' chimneys. Some of the settlers' doors might not open again for days.

They were a strange and lazy lot, their Masters. Some were indentured servants, paying for their passage with several years of labor. But many others were former noblemen and landed gentry, the second-born, non-inheriting sons of wealthy families. The men often avoided hard work in favor of long, haranguing debates and arguments over how to tame the land and which of them held greater claims to hereditary title.

To a man, they had sailed to this faraway place not to become farmers, but to satisfy a lust for instant wealth even more fierce than the greed of their Spanish foes. Each dreamed of seizing gold from the natives and sailing home to the Old Country as wealthy men, their wildest fantasies fulfilled.

The Animals? They were simply there for labor and food.

The beasts knew that the next time they would see a settler's face would probably be in the commission of a specific, dastardly act. Hatchet in hand, some red-cheeked human would be glimpsed scurrying through the cold to snatch one of Hoss' feathered friends, carry off the poor beast, and slaughter it.

The memory filled him with horror. It always had.

A rooster's angry cluck caught his ear. He looked over to see the bird flaring his feathers in a threatening posture, facing down one of his rivals across the feeding trough. There lay a single  kernel of corn, solitary and pathetic. A dot of enticing yellow amid dirt and bits of straw.

It was the last food for the day, and probably for a long, good while.

An hour before, he had watched desperate Animals converge on the trough, which was actually no more than a channel in the ground. The men had tossed out several handfuls of dried out grain with less care than they would have used emptying an overfilled bedpan. Gander's heart had broken to see once proud barnyard Animals scratching and clawing as if it were a king's feast.

Now the beasts had sunk even further, watching two of the barn's most fierce and majestic patriarchs facing off to duel over a solitary kernel.

Suddenly, the pair leaped at each other and began slashing in a frenzy of feathers and blood. A great gasp went up from the nearby Animals. Surely, one of the roosters would soon die for that one morsel.

As Hoss and the others stood watching the battle in horror, Gander, the goose, rushed forward and hurled his body between the two combatants.

"Stop this!" he honked. "It's not worth it!"

Maddened by hunger, neither bird showed the least regard for his heroism. Gander tried to deflect their vicious pecks, but a lunging beak struck his vulnerable left knee. Blood spurted. His legs buckled. Gander fell to the ground, wincing in agony. At last, the two crazed roosters backed away from each other, the spell of their rage broken.

At once Gander's mate Gloria and his children were at his side, tending to his wounds and comforting him with loud cries of concern.

"Can you stand?" asked Gloria, her voice wracked with anxiety. Even here in the barn, a goose who could not walk would not survive long. The Masters would quickly notice and dispatch him to…

No Animal cared to dwell much on those matters.

But Gander struggled to a standing position, grimaced with effort and pain, and remained upright—although a bit crooked.

"I can stand," he announced in his bravest voice.

"But Daddy, can you walk?" asked his young gosling.

He extended his good leg forward and the wounded one bore his weight, quivering badly. But it held.

"I can walk."

A great cheer went up. Gander smiled gratefully. He was generally respected, with a friendly and caring personality that had made him a favorite among all the species.

Hoss, who had watched helplessly from his horse's height, shook his head in dismay. He loved his fellow beasts dearly, and it pained him to see them endure such degrading conditions. The sight of those majestic roosters tearing each other apart, and then maiming a valued friend, tore at his gut. A bitter thought swept through him.

*Something had to change.*

After the Animals returned to their stalls and coops, Hoss remembered a dream which had lingered in his thoughts all day. Although it had been unusually moving and vivid, he had not considered it anything more than just another odd product of his imagination.

That is, until this moment.

As he pondered the dream's meaning, a dark and frightening thought came to him. After two years of drought, this winter could prove far worse than even the past grueling cold seasons. Worse still, dryness was not the only cause of this crisis. The Masters' incompetence had played a key role. More interested in pursuing gold than farming, they had neglected their crops and dallied their way into looming disaster.

At once, everything fell into place within him. The dream, the sense of doom and danger—all converged into a single, dazzling realization.

Hoss neighed gently and began to glance from side to side. With a low snicker and a long nod of his great head, he summoned his fellow horse Speedy. Though the settlers called him Black Jack, all the Animals referred to him as Speedy because of his high strung nature. After a few seconds, the pair stood nose to nose.

"Please tell everyone that we meet tonight," Hoss whispered softly. "This will be a special gathering. Everyone must be there. Tell them I believe our creator has given me a vision of great peril ahead. And a challenge."

The other horse's eyes grew wide with anticipation and he trotted away into the stable's shadows. The first Animal he encountered was Gander, still gamely forcing himself to walk. Speedy bent down and whispered Hoss' call. Despite his own personal crisis, Gander perked up at the news and began chattering rapidly to first his family, then anyone who would listen.

Behind him, Hoss began to hear the tiniest of murmurs grow gradually louder, then spread out through the rafters, the crannies, the stable's hidden aeries.

Before long, his ears brought to him the distant sound of clipped wings flapping and the pattering of tiny feet on straw. The rest of the geese and ducks had waddled over, numbering over a dozen.

Soon, Hoss looked around and saw his mate Hessie standing beside their twin foals Jaxon and Jevin. Even from a distance, he could see that familiar look of challenge in her eyes, the one she always flashed him when he interrupted her motherly duties. It usually meant, *honey, this had better be important…*

Behind Libby the hen—who considered herself at the top of the pecking order, no matter the species—waited the settlement's thirty chickens. All looked up at Hoss with soft clucking sounds. Even in the half-light, he could see their necks twitching forward in their familiar habit. The comical reflex, to Hoss's mind, had always made it seem as though the fowl were anticipating the inevitable slice of a Master's axe.

Tonight, however, Hoss could not muster any amusement at the notion. Instead, he shook his head, as though chasing the thought from his mind.

The stable's doors pried open with a squeak. It was Buster and the settlement's five other dogs, their ears rigid with curiosity. The hounds padded in with looks of anticipation and sat behind the chickens, panting vapor with every breath. Then came the cows, lumbering from side to side as they walked, still chewing the last of the day's meager cud.

A number of the Animals met here in the evenings following the Masters' nightly disappearance. Usually, they gathered to exchange complaints about the humans' treatment, their laziness and gross incompetence. After the latest outrages and Master-gossip had all been shared, they would sing beloved old barnyard songs from the Old Country. Gander himself had launched the meetings long before, to foster a spirit of community and improve morale among the diverse species who lived and slaved and died together during the day.

This night, however, was different. That was clear from the piercing gleam in Hoss' eyes and in the lack of laughter or mirth in the air. A strange, expectant quiet hung over them all.

"Are we all here?" Hoss asked at last.

He looked around at the crowd of twitching, wide-eyed Animal life stretched out before him. The horses' face hung suspended in the gloom over all the others, watching from nearby stalls.

"I'm still waiting on my brother Norm," called Gill the pig from the middle of the pack.

"Of course," grumbled Hoss amiably. "He's probably curled up on his owner's hearth, thinking he's become some kind of house pet."

An old bull named Julius grumbled behind them. "Someone needs to remind that pig that he's still liable to wind up as someone's breakfast bacon, one of these mornings."

"I'll get him," offered Buster with a soft, good-natured growl. The dog hurried out into the night.

"I have a bone to pick with you," Gill said to Hoss, with a dark look and a burst of his strong, commanding voice. The pigs were all known for being skilled speakers and unusually gifted in human-logic. "You make fun of we pigs working so hard to be loved by our Masters. But you know we have more at stake than all of you. Do I need to remind everyone of the facts we all know so well?"

"Not really," began Hoss, but his rejoinder was drowned out by Gill, who was too worked up to await a reply.

"We aren't born with anything to offer the Masters until the day we die. Unlike you, Hoss, we were not endowed with a huge frame made for great labor. And unlike you, Libby, we don't lay eggs, or give milk like you cows."

"I apologize," Hoss said with a good-natured snort. "I didn't mean anything insulting."

Just then, Buster reappeared with a red-flushed porker in tow.

"Sorry, everyone," Norm muttered.

"We understand," Hoss said in his most sympathetic tone. "Gill and I were just discussing why you pigs have to work harder than most of us on your Master friendships."

Gill shot Hoss a sharp, questioning glance, as though wondering if the horse was going to continue the argument. Hoss only shook his head disarmingly.

"I came as fast as I could," Norm huffed, finally taking his place next to the long row of his own large family. "I heard something important was afoot."

"I believe it is," Hoss replied. "And thank you for making such great effort to be here."

At last, Hoss looked out and drank in the scene of all the assembled Animals. At the sight of them all crowded together, large and small, feathered and furred, Hoss felt a great surge of affection for his long time companions. Like him, they had been good-natured, hard-working beasts, uncomplaining of their lot, tolerant and truly caring towards each other. The Animals all knew that they sustained the inept settlers, sparing them even worse famine and starvation than their carelessness had already caused.

But all that was changing. Today's incident with Gander was not the first: several pigs and one poor chicken had already lost eyes and limbs to the fight for dwindling food and the cracking of Masters' whips. Shortage was causing them to turn against each other, resulting in not only bruised relationships, but battered bodies. It could not continue.

Some inner certainty told Hoss, in a final confirmation, that he was doing the right thing. This poor, down-trodden bunch deserved better.

"My brothers and sisters," he began, "I believe I have been given a dark warning for all of us. As you know, winter has just arrived, three weeks late by my reckoning, which means it will be more bitter than usual."

A restless stir swept over the assembly, for Hoss' assessment of coming weather was widely considered reliable, and strongly to be heeded.

"You may ask, how could it be worse than last year? That is a worthy question. Let me say it plainly. Our Masters are in a famine, and they have ceased using our labor for planting. Their crops have failed. They are in a state of pure survival. Instead of being kept to work the land, as before, most of us face having our throats cut sometime during this winter, then being skinned and roasted for our Masters' barren tables. Without a dramatic change, none of us may live to see the spring!"

At that statement, all stirring immediately stopped. Every eye fixed itself unblinkingly on the somber-faced stallion.

Many of the smallest chicks and goslings started whimpering loudly and weeping at the blunt words. Glaring furiously at Hoss, Jada the duck, Libby the hen, and several other mothers flew onto their young ones and tried to shield their tender ears with their wings. It was a tradition among the farm Animals to withhold from their youngest the cruel knowledge of their eventual fate. Most of them learned it upon reaching maturity, or an accidental peek at the killings themselves, right there in the courtyard. This awareness became a somber cloud which would follow every one of them, every moment of their lives.

"Mothers, I apologize for frightening the young ones. But I truly believe the time for mincing words has long passed. In exchange for our lives and the product of our work, we have always assumed that the Masters would provide us certain things in exchange—things like food, shelter and safety, even relative comfort. But this winter, that understanding has all changed. We are now fighting over food. Our Masters are struggling for their own lives, and are far too preoccupied with mere survival to worry about ours. We are no longer valued assets for them to cherish. We are nothing more than meat."

Gill reared back his head from the back row and called out.

"So what do you propose we do about this? Or did you just gather us to frighten us out of our wits?"

"That is a fair question," Hoss replied. "Because I do, in fact, have good news. I had a dream last night, and it was incredibly vivid. In my sleep, I saw a wondrous vision of life as it could be for all of us. We all lived some distance from here, in a settlement of our very own. The males among us were no longer slaughtered for meat and our females kept to mate with the survivors. Each family had both a father and mother to love and raise their children. We all worked for our own betterment, not that of a human tyrant. Each family provided not only for its own needs, but had enough left over to trade with other families for necessary things. Those who were sick or unfortunate received help from the kindness of those with more, the kind of help that launched them back into productive lives. We had liberty, and the thrill of liberty led to success, and prosperity. We were masters of our own destinies. And we lived without the threat of that awful blade hanging over our necks!"

Several of the young male beasts reared back and bleated, honked, quacked, neighed and mooed their approval.

"But it gets even better. I propose to you, brothers and sisters," Hoss continued, "that what I saw was no ordinary dream. It was a true vision of what's possible. And I say we act on it. Now. Before any more of our precious lives are sacrificed to the Masters' desperation."

"But without our Masters, how will we know where and how to work?" asked Julius the bull. "Where to graze? When and how my cows should give milk? When to come in from the cold? When the hens should lay eggs, or the horses to pull a load?"

"I'd like to answer that," came Gander's voice, and the wounded goose waddled awkwardly up to the front. "Many of you still remember the farm where we lived before sailing here. Then you also recall my father Samuel. In his younger days, he was what we called *wild*. That meant he was totally on his own. Completely free. He could fly where he wanted, eat what and when he wished and swim to his heart's content in any pond that fit his fancy. He said it was the most glorious feeling you could imagine, to just spend the day following your instincts through the whole wide world, wherever the winds and your strength could take you. He told us that we were created to be free Animals.

"This all changed when, on a whim, he abandoned his normal habit of walking through tall grass to a pond, and instead took a well-worn trail. This turned out to be a mistake. A hunter had hidden a snare on the path, and Samuel's left foot became caught.

"He struggled for several days trying to free that left foot, to no avail. He bit at the snare. He pulled at it. He tried to fly away, but was always jerked back to the ground. Finally, he realized that there was no other course of action but to cut off his own limb. Fortunately, the trail was rocky and he happened to spot a piece of flint among the rocks. He held the flint in his beak and endured the horrible pain until he had cut through, first his flesh, then the tendons, and finally the bone."

While gasps of dismay swept through the assembly, Gander leaned forward and grasped a small gray object in his bill, then flipped it out into the younger crowd before him.

"Here is that very flint. I keep it around so I'll never forget how precious freedom is. It is so valuable and rare that for Samuel, it was worth more than the price of his foot, and well-worth spending the rest of his days waddling comically to one side.

"One day he flew over our farm pond, caught sight of my mother's beauty, and fell in love at first sight. She in turn, bless her heart, thought his cock-eyed walk was absolutely adorable. They loved each other so much that he decided being with her was worth giving up that precious freedom. So he let himself be tamed in order to stay by her side.

"He wound up being a patriarch on Farmer McDonald's farm, which is how most of us remember him. For him, the barnyard was a far cry from his old freedom, although Farmer McDonald's kind treatment kept most of us from understanding how he felt. Yet many of you remember how, even when he was an old geezer barely able to remember his own name, he would introduce himself as a 'free bird,' and mutter a few sentences about the wonders of liberty. He never forgot it, not until his dying day."

Accompanied by a few grunts, honks and quacks of agreement, Gander turned back and rejoined his family. Hoss again stepped to the forefront.

"Some of us as youth made fun of Samuel's old mutterings," Hoss continued, "because we didn't understand them. But now, I do. Samuel's story has something huge to tell us: that our ancestors used to be wild! That's right. Once upon a time, our kind all lived in complete freedom. That's why you cows will know when to give milk. Our Creator wrote the knowledge in our minds, and when you feel the nudge of your calves' tongues against your teats, it will all come back to you! We've become so accustomed to giving away our wealth that we've forgotten how to use it in the simple, ordinary way it was intended: for the good of our families and ourselves!"

The Animals paused to drink in these bold words, for in all the years they'd listened to Hoss' wisdom, they had never heard him say something so radical.

"So you propose we just walk out of here and into the cold night?" asked Julius at last, with an anxious tone. Several other beasts turned to him with shared, nervous looks. "You're proposing we just abandon the only shelter we have, poor as it is. That's insane!"

"It may be cold out there, as you say," said Hoss. "but my senses tell me it will soon grow far, far colder. And the Masters have little to give us. Besides, the daylight would be a far too dangerous time to escape. In numbers like ours, we would almost certainly be spotted.

"Many of you know that Master Griffith has been pulling on that brown bottle of his lately, and when he does, he sometimes leaves our door unlatched. Well, I noticed that he's done that again tonight. I have also seen how they push the bar across the palisade gate. We can push it in the other direction and open it ourselves. I say we follow the wonderful vision I was given and immediately strike out—and follow our destiny!"

"Well, I'm staying," grumbled Julius. "So is my family and any other Animal with any common sense. You all go on and die out there—I can't say we won't miss you fellows something fierce, but so be it. Hoss, you seem to have your heart set on this fool plan."

"I will miss you too," said Hoss. "Are you sure you won't reconsider?"

Julius fixed the horse with the saddest, most forlorn look any of the Animals had ever seen him muster. Then he shook his head *no*.

"I respect your decision." Now he turned to the wounded goose. "Gander, with your injury, are you wanting to make the journey?"

Gander straightened his neck with a determined look. "I can walk, if only a bit slower. And I wouldn't miss this if I had to hop on one leg."

Hoss turned back to the crowd. "Who with me chooses liberty, freedom and long life, over slavery, constant fear and certain death?"

At those irresistible words, all but Julius's family, a scattering of chickens, some cows and a few sheep, rose in a chorus of approval so overpowering that even the Masters in nearby cabins threw open a window or two to see what all the howling ruckus was about.

None of the humans dared to leave their homes and brave the cold, however, to witness what happened next.

# Chapter Two

Ironically, the fog which the Animals had once dreaded as the omen of a harsh winter wound up actually saving their whole escape plan.

It started with the barn's door, accidentally left unlatched by the incompetent settlers. The old wood slowly inched open under the nudge of a dog's moist nose. Three staring pairs of eyes appeared above his—one pig, one goose and one horse, in that order—peeking through the crack to scan the compound for signs of human activity.

Instead, their gazes found instead only fog; a luminous veil of mist which gave them only tattered, moonlit glimpses of the surrounding cabins.

But no sign of any Masters watching.

At last the door opened further and the Animals, without Julius and the other doubters, set out to face the bone-chilling air and frozen, hard-packed earth. With hardly a sound, beasts large and small trudged forward in one single-filed row. Vapors from each breath trailed their bodies like a cloud of rising souls, drifting to join the very fog that had just frightened some into staying behind.

Now hidden from prying eyes by the hazy layer around them, the trust-line of Animal marchers made its way beyond the central courtyard. Turning left at its end, they veered to the gate which marked the front of the settlement's palisade wall.

Many of the beasts, especially the young, glanced up and inwardly remarked that the barrier had never looked more towering and forbidding than at that moment, looming blue-tinged in the hazy moonlight.

At least one comforting fact gave them hope. As Hoss had expected, its latch required only the slightest nudge.

Hoss pushed the bar to the left and the gate creaked open. At the head of the pack, he did not indulge himself in a look backwards. He knew the gesture would have provoked many behind him to follow suit. His ears would have soon filled with calls of sadness, regret and second thoughts. He pushed through and stepped out, drinking in the great wildness of the vast and forbidding New World.

He had been outside the walls before, except bound by a halter and pulled by a human. Back then, being so close to that much free space had seemed such a cruel reminder of his bondage that he had forced himself to keep his head down and avoid looking at it directly. The memory caused him to twinge and recall how the whip had stung him for failing to move fast enough or grasp his Master's bidding.

Now, however, he stood and drank in a lingering eyeful. Gleaming silver under a single veil of mist and moonlight, a broad meadow stretched forward to a fringe of towering pine trees. The sight before him proved less menacing than his worst fears had pictured. In fact, it struck him as beautiful, in a cold and wintry sense.

Hoss could hear the sound of his fellow escapees filing out behind him, and then a series of gasps and soft sighs.

"Is freedom always this pretty?" asked Hessie, Hoss' mate, between puffs of breath. She, along with many of the other beasts, had not been outside the compound in months.

"I have no idea," Hoss replied. "But it is an awesome sight, isn't it?"

He tried to think of something more inspiring to say, but in the oddness of the moment it took him several seconds to even think up a decent word of encouragement.

"My fellow Animals, we go like pilgrims on to our future!" he called out at last, and proceeded forward. It was the best he could come up with.

A strange lightheadedness swam through his senses just then. He felt struck by the magnitude of what he had just done. He wondered if any group of farm Animals had ever walked away from their Masters of their own free will like this before, boldly embracing an unknown future in a cold, nighttime wilderness? It didn't feel like anything he had heard of before.

Something about his steps seemed alien. It felt as though another horse altogether was doing the walking. The ground held him up like normal soil, and the dried grasses gave way under his feet like those he remembered from the Old World. (He had to think back that far, because lately these Animals had done precious little walking on actual, living grass.) Still, something felt wrong.

Not wanting to betray his nervousness, he gave only the quickest of glances backwards to see if the line had held behind him. The sight of feathered and furry backs greeted his anxious look, glowing softly in the half-light.

*Bless them,* he thought. *They've stayed with me!*

Soon, however, Hoss felt the earth soften and ooze liquidly beneath his steps. His very next stride sank down to his ankle in cold mud laced with brown water. He looked ahead and saw moonlight shining off the wet banks. Beyond them lay stagnant ponds of what he realized, in wetter years, would have been a large river tributary stretching off into the darkness.

Clearly this discovery meant that, given normal rainfall, the Masters' settlement would have actually stood on an island. He wondered if the humans even knew that. Tonight, given the seasons' lack of moisture, it presented little more than a mucky navigation hazard.

Peering at the way ahead to spot the driest possible crossing, Hoss asked himself whether the swamp would hinder their escape or help cover their tracks. Hoping for the latter, he gingerly walked ahead.

"Stay in single file!" he called back. "And follow my steps as close as you can!"

That proved easier said than done. Before long, the slower Animals devised a solution: climbing atop the backs of some of their faster and more cooperative brethren. The dogs, endowed with swifter feet than all the others, migrated to the front of the line and scouted out a safe route through the muck. A redoubled wind assaulted their crossing of the sloshy terrain. Mercifully, they reached the relative shelter of the opposite side in a few, bone-chilling minutes.

Before long they were on dry land again, following Hoss into a dense canopy of ancient oak and pine. At first, the wall of leafy darkness frightened some of the smaller and younger Animals. With the dogs' help, however, they soon found themselves walking along an old trail, carved years ago through the thicket by either wild Animals or some native tribe.

A peaceful hush fell over the procession as the wonder of this wild beauty and the thrill of fresh discovery kept them all peering ahead for the next twist in their path. The silence thankfully extended even to the young ones, who forgot their sore legs and empty stomachs in the thrill of such a grand journey.

Under this awestruck hush, they walked for hour upon plodding hour. They hiked through dense forest and moon-dappled glade, along open meadows and fringes of woods so deep that even the keenest-eyed among them could hardly glimpse a foot inside. Somehow, they all seemed to realize that it was useless to complain, as the walk's many discomforts were afflicting them all equally .

In fact, they walked so long that some of them began to feel they were forgetting even the sight of the place they had left. It seemed as though the settlement belonged to some faraway dream, to a strangely altered existence.

Night turned into day and the sun rose on their escape. Trudging ahead, Hoss pictured the first Master stumbling into their Animal shelter for the odd egg or squeeze of milk and shouting out loud, perhaps even falling over backward at the sight of the nearly empty stalls. The thought made him snort in quiet mirth, even as it made him grateful for the miles they had already put between them and their tormentors.

They found a small pond and paused for a drink, but then continued on again despite bleats of protest from a few of the youngest. The sun grew higher in the sky, bringing relief from the cold, and then sank again without their trek having reached its end. Hoss seemed driven by his inner vision of the specific spot they had to find.

Although Hoss showed no signs of slowing, some of the procession's weaker members grew simply too exhausted to continue. Once he realized that they had put a safe distance between themselves and the settlement, he consented to halt in a small forest meadow where they could forage. There they spent a night sleeping under the stars. Thankfully, the breeze seemed gentler this night, and seemed to carry less of a chill. The moon climbed high, and within minutes the escapees shared the deep slumber of the physically exhausted.

Hoss roused them at the first glow of dawn. With hardly a murmur, the still-drowsy group swayed to its feet, reformed the line and began trudging down the trail.

It proved to be another long day of following trails ever deeper into the wilderness. The journey seemed so endless that many began to silently wonder if Hoss' promised home would ever appear.

That evening, they came to the shimmering edge of a broad body of water. Shivering under the barren canopy of branches, the Animals looked ahead impatiently. Scowling with the effort of staying warm, they fell silent for a moment.

The channel was so choked with fog that it looked like the surface of some vast, boiling cauldron. All the way to a shrouded horizon, its breadth seethed with a thousand wisps of ghost-like vapor. None of the beasts had ever known that something so lovely could feel so cold and forbidding.

"We're crossing *that*?" asked Libby, the elder hen in a dubious tone.

"I believe the place I dreamed of lies on the other side," Hoss replied softly. He walked up to the water's edge and peered forward into the mist. "I am pretty sure I see the far shore," he called back. "It's not as far as it seems."

But as soon as everyone took in the obstacle before them, a chorus of whines and laments arose.

"Is that the ocean?" cried Gill.

One of the chickens exclaimed, "That water must be near freezing! And look at that current! We'll all drown!"

"There's no way," said Bossy the cow, who then turned to Hoss with a look of disbelief. "Hoss, is this your idea of freedom and liberty? To trade a solid shelter for *this*—a freezing deathtrap?"

"Yeah!" chimed in Libby. "I'm going back!"

"So am I!" clamored a half-dozen other Animals.

Hoss shook his head sadly. "My friends, I have no wish to quarrel with you, let alone deprive you of your liberty. I am only saying that as dangerous as this path may be, we have no choice but to follow it. The land meant for us lies across these waters. It's true that the way looks dangerous, because it probably is. But isn't suffering some risk better than having our lives stolen at the point of an axe?"

"No, it isn't," said Bernard, one of the sheep. "I'm going back too."

The ram turned around and began loping back in the settlement's direction, his mate and their lone lamb following mournfully behind them. In the gloom, a dozen more Animals cast apologetic glances at Hoss and scampered along to join those turning back.

Robby the dog stepped up and gazed at Hoss with a remorseful squint. "I really prefer to keep going with you," he panted, "but these poor brothers and sisters need a guide home. Without help from someone who can sniff out the way back, I fear they will never make it. Goodbye, my friends."

With a mournful nod, he turned around and ran to catch up with the returning group.

A silence fell over those who remained.

"Maybe we can form a circle around the young to guide their way," suggested Hoss in a hopeful voice.

"Better yet, what if we horses, and maybe the cows, carry as many as will fit on our backs?" offered Speedy the young stallion.

"Of course. We have broad shoulders and haunches," said Hoss. "The geese and ducks are all strong swimmers, even if it's been awhile since you had much practice. We have enough numbers to form a protective circle around the young and less buoyant. What do you say, everybody?"

No one answered. The Animals simply stared ahead at the span, whose almost unreachable far side seemed to taunt them. Finally, a voice spoke out into the void.

"Well, it's not getting any warmer, is it?"

The voice belonged to Bruce the bull, well-known for his bluntness.

The discussion died down as Bruce's penetrating question seemed to carry the day. It became immediately clear to everyone within earshot that there was no good reason to prolong the inevitable.

"Hoss, I will go first," offered Speedy. "I'll tell you exactly how warm it is."

So with a scattering of fearful cries, the chickens, the young and the non-swimmers climbed onto the broader backs of the horses and cows. All the sheep, pigs, ducks and geese positioned themselves alongside the formation like the flanks of a ship. The females herded the young and elderly into the middle space created between them.

An anxious clamor rose from the children. The young ones did not understand the need to be huddling in such a strange manner, out in this cold and forbidding place. Their mothers bent down to reassure them, their words of comfort quavering with barely-contained apprehension.

At last, all the Animals were enclosed within the cordon of bodies, and the odd shaped group closed ranks.

"Let's go, and stay together!" whinnied Hoss, "I will bring up the rear." With that, Speedy started off at a brisk pace.

Although the water hardly slashed when Speedy stepped in, he shivered and neighed loudly when it reached his haunches. Hoss somberly watched Hessie and his sons precede him into the water. The youngest ones' cries tripled in volume when the surface met their little bodies, forcing him to peer ahead with a look of apprehension. Those on his back huddled there in a furry mass, shivering as one.

"Just stay together, and focus!" one mother called out to her babies. "Keep paddling your little feet!" came one mother's cry to those swimming on their own. The instruction was taken up by a dozen other parents. The refrain of "keep paddling!" echoed across dozens of terrified figures.

Suddenly they broke clear of the shore's weaker current and were all riverborne at once. To someone watching from a distance, the pattern of bobbing heads would have resembled the shape of some long sea creature, gliding across the surface.

The brave Animals swam into the swirling mist and for a moment, their cries of fear gave way to sighs of awe and wonder.

The river breezes had swirled and teased the vapors into shapes suggesting gliding swans and a whole menagerie of wispy, fairy-tale apparitions. The sight struck many as more enchanting than anything they had ever seen.

But an instant later, the water brought everyone back to reality. Speedy, who in his eagerness had swum on ahead of the rest, whinnied loudly and reared up in the water. He had been broadsided by current rushing down from their right.

"Steady!" shouted Hoss. "You're losing them!"

"I'm trying!" Speedy called back. "It caught me unawares!"

A spine-chilling scream pierced the air as little bodies swept from his back.

"Gwen! Arnold!" shrieked a hen's voice. "Catch them!"

Hoss now reached the current himself, an abrupt plunge of water previously hidden by the mist. Warned by Speedy's plight, he had turned his shoulders into the flow and plowed into it furiously, as though galloping through a wall of mud.

It wasn't enough. Although Hoss stayed upright, the rest of their carefully held formation flew apart in one wild, numbing instant of fear and chaos. Gwen and Arnold's father, a chicken and a non-swimmer, jumped from Bruce's back to try to save the children. He plunged beneath the surface and disappeared. Hoss recognized Gander's voice, honking frantically to non-swimmers disappearing all around him.

On every side, the water churned with the Animals' struggle against a strengthening current. More screams rang out, accompanied by sounds of tiny lungs gulping and gurgling for air. Gander swam to the little ones' aid and pushed several up onto Bruce's broad back.

Hoss risked a careful glance downstream, anxious not to toss his own passengers into the river. He winced in horror, then turned forward again to gauge the crossing's progress.

They were barely a fourth of the way across. Just then, Speedy unleashed an ear-splitting scream of pain and thrashed upwards in the water.

"My leg hit a sharp rock!" Speedy moaned. "I have to turn back!"

"But the others need you," Hoss insisted. "We have to stay in formation, or more will be lost!"

"I'm sorry, but I'm exhausted, and I can't even move my leg! I have to go back!"

"Hoss, take me with you!" came the voice of one chicken clinging to Speedy's back.

"Yes" drifted another. "My family too!"

Three chicken families latched themselves to Hoss' flowing mane and tail and refused to let go. The others on Speedy's back had endured enough. They clamored to return to the nearer shore.

With that, Speedy wrenched his massive neck and turned himself around in the water. The current caught him more powerfully than he seemed to have bargained for. For a moment it did not seem he would gain the momentum to return. Finally, with loud groans of effort, he managed to reverse his direction and labor back.

"Please if we can just keep moving forward," Hoss called out to the others, "I think we can…"

He tried to stay aware of Speedy's progress, but the effort of staying afloat proved far too urgent.

It was the last time they would ever see the young stallion or any of the last-minute returnees.

Just then disaster struck again, as though intent on one final blow. Hoss had rescued several struggling swimmers who, in their desperation, had clamped their beaks and feet onto his tail and slowed his progress. Now his front hooves, straining furiously beneath the water, struck the same submerged boulder which had ended Speedy's journey. The impact pulled his chest and neck downward and peppered his back with the awful sensation of little feet lifting free from their holds.

Hoss felt engulfed by an overpowering refusal to accept this fate. He stilled his limbs for a moment and allowed the current to pull him past the chicks. Then he lowered his head onto the water's surface and caught their bodies against the length of his neck. When they all rested against him, he began swimming again, harder than ever before. But by then, he had drifted far downstream. All the others had vanished from sight. Two questions shot through him like a lightning bolt—

—*had they made it or not? Could he swim the extra distance necessary to make the shore?*

As he struggled, he looked ahead. Somehow, despite all of his efforts, the opposite bank had not grown much closer. Determination now surged within him, reanimating his limbs. He simply had to catch up with those who were now out of sight.

Summoning up reserves of energy he never knew he had, the stallion numbly forced his limbs into motion and ignored the pain in his leg. Shutting his eyes, he simply clamped his mind around a single goal…

*One more lunge.*

*One more push.*

With every ounce of his remaining strength, he bore down on the simple task of keeping those long legs straining forward. The final yards crawled by in a misery of gnawing cold and fatigue.

Finally, his agony grew so intense that the great horse finally saw his world blacken and his senses start to abandon him.

Onshore, a cluster of beleaguered Animals lay panting and shuddering around a large rock which jutted from an unlikely spot on the muddy bank. Although the common emotion was one of relief and gratitude for simply having survived, a plaintive cry also ran through the exhausted bodies—especially those of Hessie and her two colts.

*Where is Hoss?*

Traumatized and grief-stricken, the Animals dreaded losing a leader like him. Hoss had been their emotional and physical beacon during this terror, guiding their way towards life itself. Besides: he was the driving force behind this whole journey. They could not survive losing him.

For several long moments, a sizable number of the escaped beasts stood upon the shoreline, craning necks and shoulders for a sight of their brave leader through the fog. Behind them came the heartbreaking sound of weeping mothers and fathers caring for their young ones and counting the toll of those who had disappeared.

At last, the old workhorse's familiar broad shoulders and long head lifted slowly through the current. A great cheer went up.

Hoss was returning to them!

As he approached, the cheers redoubled. His great muzzle and flank held drenched passengers and seven half-drowned youngsters rescued from the current.

However, the Hoss who greeted their welcome and nuzzled the shore was not the same powerful Animal who had set out from the other side. As proud as he was, the exhausted stallion could do little more than roll himself onto the mud beside the rock at the water's edge. His chest heaved with loud, frighteningly hoarse gasps of breath.

For a moment it seemed he would never stop lying there sucking in mouthfuls of air, seemingly weaker and more vulnerable than anyone could ever remember seeing him. Unable to calm his breathing, Hessie stood and nudged his cheek with her velvet muzzle.

His sons stood back with shocked expressions. They too, had never seen their formidable father so helpless.

Finally, Gill and the others walked to his side and began trying to coax him up with their own haunches. Gander waddled over and gently prodded the hero's nose with his beak.

"You have to make it," Gander implored. "We need you!"

Hoss fixed him with a bleary look. "How many made it?" he whispered.

"I think the count is forty-six," Gander replied. "Sixty-four set out. We lost eighteen. Forney and Dodge perished trying to save Emmy and Waddle. Gwen and Arnold's father died trying to save them. Most of the rest were little ones. My own Ben is missing."

Hoss' eyes closed slowly. Whether they did so from grief or sheer tiredness was any Animal's guess.

"But we made it," Gander said, bending over and repeating even louder. "We're on the other side, and just like you said, we're free! Do you understand? We're completely free!"

At that moment a gosling believed lost wriggled out of the river. Shivering like some animated feather-ball, he saw his sad-faced mother and hopped over to her breast.

"Ben!" Gloria, Gander's mate cried. Gander let out a loud whoop of joy.

With that, Hoss smiled and let his eyelids slowly droop shut.

# Chapter Three

The solemn closing of those large brown eyes sent a wave of sorrow and disbelief breaking over those gathered around Hoss' prone figure. Once again, Hessie leaned down and nuzzled his cheek with a mournful gentleness. His brother Champ approached from the other side and prodded under his neck, as though trying to push the thick workhorse back onto his feet. Gander inserted his long neck into the fray, took a good look and announced, "He's still with us! Brothers and sisters, let's warm him up!"

With a chorus of varied calls and exclamations, the Animals converged onto their leader. Large and small, feathered and furry alike burrowed into Hoss' chilly flanks, forming a colorful and diverse blanket over him.

For several long, frozen moments, it seemed cruel silence would rule the day. Gander wriggled along Hoss' back, trying to press himself closer and impart all the warmth he could. Champ buried his nose under Hoss' neck, trying to raise it from the cold ground.

Nothing happened. The Animals lay silent upon him, wishing against all hope that their efforts would not be in vain.

"Noooo…," Hessie whimpered imploringly.

Far above and indifferent to their grief, the fog's last strips parted to reveal a pale, crescent moon. A cold wind moaned, unbroken by any other sound.

At last, just as they were about to give up, one of Hoss' long eyelashes quivered. Both eyelids parted gradually and peeked apart. His ears perked forward as one.

"Thank you," he whispered.

"Don't exert yourself," Hessie replied. "Save your strength."

His gaze met hers, and he lifted his head to take in the scene.

"No, I have to keep moving. And we all need to. We must put more distance between ourselves and this cold place. And keep warm as the night grows colder."

So, with a mumbled apology to the friends draped all about him, Hoss struggled back to his feet, drooping and slow. Finally upright, he glared back over at the treacherous river.

"If it wasn't for the hope of freedom, I don't think I would have made it," he said weakly.

"I don't think any of us would have," Gander rejoined. Then his voice grew husky with emotion. "In a way, this odd rock marks the spot of our first steps as truly free Animals."

"Freedom Rock it is, then," Hoss said.

They stood silent, appreciating how perfect the stone's new name sounded.

"I'll never forget this place," Hoss said. "We are now all free and equal. We can choose our own destiny."

And then he turned, beckoning with the motion of his head, and with a slower gait than ever before, trudged forward into the forest. An odd mixture of dread, excitement and exhaustion seemed to settle over the others.

For a short distance they plodded forward through an ever-thickening, moonlit underbrush, alert to every nighttime sound, growing utterly still at every new sight and bend in their path.

Finally, just as it seemed the last of their strength was almost spent, Buster the dog came bounding back from one of his frequent scouting missions.

"Guess what, everyone!" he panted, grinning broadly. "Just a few hundreds yards ahead, I found a whole cluster of large, well-built shelters in a clearing! Without hesitating, I risked my life to check out each structure with my sense of smell. They used to be lived in by humans a long time ago, but they're now completely empty. They've been that way for some time."

At the news, Hoss snorted a loud prayer of thanks and bolted forward in his eagerness. The Animals followed Buster, who was so excited that he ran on ahead and lost them several times, all the way to a broad meadow gleaming eerily in the moonlight.

There, as promised, stood a ring of rounded huts, their smooth sides covered with birch bark.

The Animals stood as though dumbstruck before the sight, unable to believe that such a perfect place could simply have lain there waiting for them,

"Is this the place you saw in your vision?" Gander asked Hoss.

Hoss did not reply with words but with a bleary-eyed, affirming nod of his head.

"I can hardly believe it," he said at last. "It is, but I did not believe the Creator would prove so true to what He showed me. This is it, my friends. Our very own colony, not of master and slave, but of free and equal citizens. Yes: Animal Colony. Let's make that its name."

There was a pause, but then several Animal voices were heard, saying the name slowly, tentatively.

*Animal Colony. Animal Colony.*

A low rumble came from the group. Hoss knew them too well to mistake its meaning. They liked the name. It was all the debate they would need.

"So now, let us take possession."

With that, the shivering Animals crept ahead and peered into the clean, well-insulated homes which lay ready for them in the heart of a dangerous wilderness.

"Find your own shelters, friends," called out Hoss, his hoarse voice betraying that he was at the ultimate end of his strength, "And stay warm. We'll gather in the morning and speak again."

And so species by species, family by family, the Animal escapees from the human settlement nosed their way into their respective homes, huddled together for warmth, and against all odds, survived their third frigid night of well-earned liberty.

The next morning dawned fair and cold, and with no sign of the village's new inhabitants. Although none of the Animals were eager to leave the warmth of their shelters to face the chill, another motive eventually forced them out, starting with the smallest among them: the chickens, ducks and geese.

That driving force was hunger.

The gnawing stomachs which had helped persuade them to leave their Masters had only grown emptier following nights of hiking, swimming chilled waters and raging fear.

As a result, the cluster of early-risers which gathered amidst the brightening dawn of that first day did not have the joys of freedom on its mind. Before long, the dogs had joined their bird brethren in a frantic search around the buildings' perimeter. Minutes into their sniffing, Buster began furiously pawing at the ground just outside their circle, thinking he had found some kind of buried food cache.

A minute later, those watching reared back with sharp calls of alarm and disgust. Others came to see what was the matter and several of them turned back, nauseated.

The pawing had unearthed five human skeletons, half-clothed, their bones still strung with decomposed flesh. Headbands and tattered feathers hung from their skulls.

All the Animals knew that the time for reburying the dead had come in earnest. Even those not ideally suited for the task joined their canine friends in returning the soil over the deceased.

"Look at this!" called out Gill a few moments later. His dirt-stained snout, usually kept fastidiously clean, was now pushing around a half-dozen wooden implements. "Digging tools and a wooden plow! This is unbelievable, as though they were left for us!"

Gill's discovery, however remarkable, was actually ignored, for in the next second a dog's howl of delight rang out from the opposite side of the clearing.

"Food!" Buster barked. "I've found grain!" And with a loud clamor of calls, all the waking Animals swarmed over to the hole over which he stood. The chickens, ducks and most of the geese began jumping into the depression, their beaks already pecking the air in anticipation of a long-overdue feast.

"Wait!" called out a low, powerful voice.

All the heads turned. It was Hoss, finally roused from his long, recuperative slumber and walking over to the scene.

"What is it?" asked Libby, the hen. "We're all starving, Hoss, so please hurry."

"Have we found any other food around here?" Hoss asked, finally reaching the hole's edge.

"No, this is it," replied Buster.

"Then please listen, everybody. I'm just a dumb old horse, but I know that winter is just around the corner, if not already here. It seems to me that if we can just sacrifice now and save this grain until spring, we could plant the seed then and have even more food in the future. If we eat the grain now, we will have nothing to plant, and we'll suffer more in years to come."

"I disagree," said Norm. "This grain is as much a gift to us today as the shelters were to us in the cold of the night. We've just started searching. Surely more grain will turn up as we keep exploring."

*Yeah!* rose a honking and clucking chorus from the fowl.

"Besides," added Libby, "it's been a long time since we ate much more than foraged grass and seeds. We're starving; especially our young ones. It makes no sense at all to find a blessing like this and then just sit on it."

"I think it makes all the sense in the world," said Hoss. "And consider this: if you were able to find enough to stay alive on our journey, not to mention the dusty corners of that human settlement, just think how much more we'll discover in these vast, virgin forests. Especially when we're all working together, each adding our own talents and strengths to the search!"

From their impatient stares and shaking heads, it became clear that Hoss' wisdom, usually heeded, might not prevail on that morning. They were hungry, and food was staring them in the face.

"I'll tell you what," he offered in a sad tone, "since each of our voices is equally valuable, let's take a vote on what should be done. In fact, let's agree together that as a core value of Animal Colony, whenever we must find agreement on something important, we will take a vote and abide by the will of a majority."

The Animals all thought for a second and then, turned to each other with appraising glances. The idea seemed to strike everyone favorably.

"I vote yes!" called out Gill. And a clamor of universal affirmation rose after him, almost in response.

"All right, then," said Hoss. "Who is in favor of eating this stash of grain right now, distributing it to the whole Colony for breakfast?"

As anticipated, all of the sheep, and most of the fowl, bobbed their heads *yes*.

"And who votes to safeguard it until spring, when we'll use it to plant a renewable crop? And in the meantime, work together to find food for everyone in the forests around us?"

The remainder of the Animals indicated their assent. Hoss counted carefully with nods of his head.

"The nays have it," he said at last. "We will keep the grain safe and dry, and plant it when spring comes."


That is how, in the thick of a chaotic and urgent situation, Animal Colony embraced the notion of voting on key decisions. The practice would eventually prove a cornerstone for everything that followed in the Animals' journey towards self-government.

Better still, the vote in question proved a wise one. The days that followed, although filled with relief and joy, also turned brutally cold. Soon, they had stretched into the unmistakable reality of a brutal winter, right on schedule. Indeed, had the Animals consumed the hidden grain in that early rush of hunger, they would have likely starved during the following years. Hoss' moment of life-saving caution became ingrained, along with so many other examples, in the memory of the older Animals—especially its mature mothers.

In fact, Animal Colony's first season would actually belong to the females. They took ownership of their newfound dwellings, lining their bare earth floors with leaves and underbrush, tirelessly burrowing them out to create better protection from the piercing winds. While they labored the days away, they also dispatched their males outside—no votes of approval here, for families are never democracies—to forage for more insulation and food. But the males' search around the compound proved disappointing. Digging around the village, they found little more than a few caches stuffed with bags of concave circular discs adorned with small holes and beads. Seeing no useful purpose in these, they simply put them aside.

Over time, as the Animals realized they could not simply sit in the village expecting someone to bring them food, they started to explore the surrounding forest. The meager foods they managed to turn up during those winter months came through a blend of self-determination and cooperation. Dire hunger produced in the Animals a never-before-seen ingenuity, a keen inventiveness and initiative. The threat of starvation forced each species to clearly evaluate their relative strengths as food-gatherers, then insert those into the group's evolving food-gathering strategy. Without being prompted or instructed, the Animals naturally began to consult each other. An elaborate scheme of mutual dependence began to emerge.

This meant that the dogs, with their keen senses of smell and talent for wide-ranging exploration, tracked miles of woods to discover prime foraging spots. They returned and bartered their help in guiding the others to the destinations for eggs and milk. The pigs, with their sensitive snouts and willingness to root through earth, further refined the search for roots, worms, and grubs beneath winter's outer shell. Hoss and the horses, along with a few sheep and cows, became transporters of their smaller brethren to and from the spots in question in return for food.

Even with the group effort, the Animals spent most of their hours trying to stay warm in their shelters and living on a meager subsistence diet. Many died from exhaustion, exposure, and starvation. But most survived that first winter as free Animals—as Hoss never failed to remind every one.

Gradually, after what seemed like the longest winter in memory, the weather began to warm. The winds grew more forgiving and in time, the first sprouts of new grass made their timid, hopeful appearance. As leaves emerged and the forest greened about them, the Animals discovered that they had inherited a beautiful patch of forest indeed.

The hungry Animals now found a new source of foraged sustenance: the green shoots peeking through the packed gray earth which had lain underfoot since their arrival. Even though it did not amount to a great deal of food, the new growth seemed to dispel the fear of starvation which had hung over them all winter. The very sight of its emerald color, peeking through like a carpet underfoot, restored everyone's hope for the future.

One morning, Hoss looked about him, took a long whiff of the warming air and the new scents on the breeze, and neighed loudly for everyone's attention.

"My friends, I think the time has come to plant the seeds we've kept at such a great price."

The statement was greeted by grateful, nodding heads and a low murmur of approval.

"All right: we horses will plow the fields and get them ready for planting. Who will take the job of removing any rocks and then bringing the grain out to the fields?" Many nodded in agreement. "After a few days, we'll need all those who can place the seeds in the furrows to take their turn. As the corn grows, we'll then need everyone to help pull any weeds. Then we will have a glorious harvest to get us through next winter with full stomachs and seed corn to plant next spring. Who is with me?"

A great cheer went up as everyone agreed to pitch in.

After the horses had done the plowing, Hoss asked other Animals to do their parts. The sheep and pigs were supposed to find and then carry away any stones the plows had brought to the surface.

For the first few hours, they all went at this task with great eagerness. By mid day, however, there was less enthusiasm and fewer Animals working in the fields. Finally, Hoss had to tell the few still working that they had accomplished enough, even though it was far short of the pristine field they had all envisioned.

The next day brought the turn of the chickens, ducks and geese to plant each kernel in furrows the horses had plowed. They also went at the task with great enthusiasm for the first hour or so.

Then, again, the work slowed to a crawl.

Issues soon surfaced. The fowl had decided that since they were more suited to eating grain than planting it, they should be allowed to eat one piece and then plant one piece. A majority of them voted to implement this benefit. And so, over Hoss' objections, it was finally conceded.

The result was a stony field bearing a much smaller crop than what was hoped for.

By the time summer arrived in earnest, the corn stalks had already started their climb towards the sky, partially filling the once empty Indian field with skimpy rows of bright green. Everyone grew excited except for Hoss.

"Yes, the corn is growing, but so are the weeds," he warned. "In fact, I'm concerned that they are actually outgrowing the corn. We all are going to have to pitch in to save the crop."

The summer days grew miserably hot, and Hoss' refrain became a nuisance to the others. As he made his rounds trying to recruit Animals to work the field, excuses began to mount.

"My foot hurts!"

"I didn't sleep well last night!"

"I'm chewing my cud; how am I supposed to pull weeds while I'm chewing my cud?"

"It's too hot today. I'll help tomorrow."

When they did show up in anemic numbers, far more energy was expended in bickering than in actual fieldwork. Most of the chickens and geese complained of having to do all the hard labor during hot summer months while the pigs and other Animals watched, ate, or played games. The cows complained of having to give up their milk to feed the dogs and pigs. The chickens felt mistreated because of having to give up their eggs and still work in the fields.

Hoss did everything he could to calm the uproar and remind every Animal that they were all in it together. Even though each faction promised to work harder and stop complaining, he still found it nearly impossible to talk many Animals into pulling weeds and tending the crop during the hot summer days.

Finally, Hoss gave up on the notion of gathering any significant help. His family and Gander's and a few others simply rose early, before the sun grew too harsh, and did their best to stay ahead of the weeds by themselves.

Within days, it became clear that their valiant effort would fail. By the end of the growing season, the once promising fields contained more weeds than corn. The bountiful crop Animal Colony could have enjoyed simply did not exist.

When fall came, Hoss found it difficult to find Animals to help harvest the grain. The same, small group always seemed to be laboring away, while the majority spent their time exchanging excuses. "We're too short to reach the ears," complained the ducks. "I have six chicks at home. Who will watch them?" complained one hen. "I just had a lamb," said one ewe, "and I don't know who the father is, I need to watch him." "I'll help with the harvest tomorrow," said Norm. "I'll feel more like working then."

Finally, after the harvest was brought in, Hoss gathered the Animals. Standing beside the under-sized pile, he addressed the throng. "Colonists, what we've saved is so modest that I'm afraid most of it will again have to be stored until next spring's planting."

This suggestion raised a fresh uproar.

"What? You mean we worked for nothing?" shouted Gill over all the others. "For a promise of some future reward? This was supposed to feed us!"

"But we didn't work hard enough to save the crop from the weeds!" Hoss insisted. "We're dealing with the aftermath of a disaster we created ourselves!"

"What do you mean we didn't work hard enough?" Gill called out angrily. "I worked. My family worked. Most everybody I know worked."

"Perhaps for an hour at a time," answered Hoss. "But saving a crop takes considerably more labor than that."

"I see a crop right in front of us," countered Gill. "And I think we should divide it evenly between all of the Colony's citizens, just as we all understood. You yourself said we are all equal."

"Now wait: we should divide evenly based on an Animal's size..." Hoss began, but his voice was drowned out in a clamor of hungry voices. The group was finished listening. The Animals simply surged forward, ready to engulf the pile of grain.

True to form, Gill made certain that every family took home an equal share. Within minutes, it was all gone.

# Chapter Four

During the winter that followed, the colonists paid a tragic price for the wasted harvest. Many of the cows and horses suffered horribly. Some, even in Hoss' extended family, starved to death. Most of the cows stop producing milk because of the meager rations.

In an effort to ease some of the suffering, Gander and a few of the other fowl shared rations with some of the larger Animals, but it was far from enough. No one but the most thrifty and conservative escaped the hunger of the season. Everyone blamed Hoss for the fact that they were in such dire straights. There was even talk of finding a new leader. Those who had done most of the work resented those who had not, yet ended up with more food than they needed. Those who had food spent most of their time guarding what they had. Instead of a spirit of cooperation and sharing, the Colony saw its first wave of crime as some stole from others, out of desperation or greed.

The great Animal Colony experiment seemed to have failed. Its bright vision and enthusiasm evaporated. Hoss' hope that every Animal would toil to benefit the group had simply not worked.

One morning in late winter, Hoss took an early morning stroll through the Colony. Once again, the village clearing had reverted to its grey and barren self. And yet more than that seemed wrong. The Colony seemed to be missing something invisible, something essential. Glancing at the lack of young playing about, sensing the absence of laughter as well as an appalling gloom hanging over their dwellings, Hoss had a key insight.

Perhaps, one reason they had been more joyfully busy after first arriving at Animal Colony was that everyone had been responsible for providing their own food.

One key change might save them from the consequences of their own, self-seeking natures. And he finally had an idea what it was.

That afternoon, he gathered his friends Gander, Gill, and his brother, Champ at the Colony's center.

"What lessons can we learn from last year's crop failure?

"I don't know about lessons learned," Gander shrugged, "but I still wonder why only a few would work yet everyone felt they deserved an equal share of the food produced."

"So the lesson," said Hoss, "is that an Animal who refuses to work, should not eat."

Everyone nodded.

"Hoss, did you notice what happened," asked Champ, "when you told the female fowl that they were exempt from fieldwork if they had chicks or ducklings to take care of?"

"Certainly," he replied. "Our hatchling population skyrocketed. The female fowl started hatching their eggs instead of trading them."

"I always thought there was a lesson in that," Gander offered. "Whatever behavior we reward seems to increase."

"And I'd imagine the opposite is also true," offered Hoss. "Whatever actions we penalize will surely decrease."

"Here's something else," offered Gill. "You told us that we are all free and equal. I think many of our brothers and sisters who had felt downtrodden their whole lives had a hard time believing they deserved equality."

"You're right, Gill," Gander said. "Equal opportunity for everyone has to be one of our foundations. We all have the same rights and freedoms, and those have to translate into equal opportunity."

Champ frowned and whinnied softly. "Opportunity, yes," he said. "But the outcome has to depend on how hard the individual works."

Hoss nodded, adding, "I have to admit, I've been discouraged by what I've seen. What we've experienced is not what our Creator showed me in my vision. We have Animals' work benefiting those who will not work. By trying to be fair to everyone, we've destroyed the natural incentive to work and benefit from our own labors. Our generosity has become crippling. Can we agree that sharing all things in common hasn't worked?"

Without a moment's hesitation, the friends nodded their common agreement.

"Then maybe," Hoss continued, "we should try giving everyone the freedom to succeed or fail on their own. Everyone can have an equal opportunity to actually prosper. They can truly own things for themselves. And every Animal's labor will directly benefit them and their family."

"I propose that we suggest a rule-change to the Colony," said Gander.

All but Gill nodded agreement.

"So here are the new principles," Gander continued, rolling his eyes in his head as he fought to remember them perfectly. "First, any Animal who refuses to work should not eat. Second, everyone deserves an equal opportunity. Third, the harvest belongs to those who toil for it. And fourth, whatever behavior we reward will increase, and whatever we punish or penalize will decrease. Is that what you were looking for?"

Hoss thought for a minute and finally nodded.

"It is. I think, if we all keep these things in mind, especially the younger generations, we can keep alive the spark that brought us here. We must agree, as Colony leaders, to never forget our responsibility to others.

Especially, we must think of ourselves as servants and never as masters."

"Aye, aye," the others said in unison.

"Let's present these to everyone this afternoon for a vote," Hoss offered. "I will make the announcement."

A few hours later the Colony gathered before Hoss, summoned there by the strong invitation of its leader and rumors of a major proclamation.

"My fellow Colonists," Hoss began in his strongest, most official sounding voice. "An important change is in order if this Colony is to overcome this cycle of hunger and neglect. I declare that the time of sharing everything equally, of everyone being given equal amounts no matter their contribution, is over. From now on, we and our families should benefit directly from our labors and be able to own our own homes and fields. No one is automatically entitled to Colony rations. It will be up to you as an individual and family to work and guarantee your own fate."

"But that's heartless!" cried out Norm along with a sizable portion of the audience. "You're throwing us out on our own!"

"No, I truly believe this will work better," Hoss argued. "More Animals will eat under this new arrangement, not fewer. You will be more motivated to work and ensure your own survival. Families will do a better job of caring for each other. Even though it sounds harsher on the surface, it is actually the kindest arrangement we can have. Consider this: can anyone now argue that the current system is working well?"

There was a great, charged silence. Even Gill found nothing to say.

Then something strange began to happen. One by one, several of the females began to vigorously nod their heads. Hoss peered forward, thinking that they were asking to speak. But when nothing was said, he realized the truth.

They were voting *no*. Soon, shamed into agreement, the majority, including Gill, did the same. The common sense in this suggestion seemed to settle over the group like the slow spreading of sunshine in the morning.

Hoss nodded gratefully.

"The change is duly agreed upon," he said. "And now, to help us remember this new state of affairs, I have four principles to present to you."

Hoss solemnly recited the propositions agreed upon earlier, and the listeners voted to enshrine them as the Colony's Four Great Truths.

Indeed, before long, it became a tradition to repeat the Great Truths in unison, every morning. Since everyone knew that their source had been the horse who had launched them on this great experiment, the phrases soon became ingrained and cherished as the Colony's philosophical backbone.

In the days that followed, Hoss declared that each family would own their present home and then would be allotted an amount of land they could handle and maintain as their own personal property.

The pride of actually owning something immediately changed the atmosphere of the Colony. The Animals started to talk about their plans for the future. They discussed which horse they would barter with to plow their field and who they would hire to help in planting, weeding and harvesting. Or, they determined to do most of the work themselves; whichever fit their abilities, character and wishes.

Before long, a new warm and fraternal spirit of cooperation developed between the Animals, one which had never existed even in the previous hardship of living under the Masters. The cows began to barter their milk to the entire Colony. And in return, every recipient made certain to give back a tangible portion from their own gifts and talents. The chickens did likewise with their eggs. And the sheep exchanged their wool to help the more coolly endowed stay warm.

Another benefit also became apparent. Chickens who had never done so willingly, now contributed some of their eggs to the hungriest of their brethren. Cows allowed some of their milk to be given out to orphaned youngsters of other species, even an elderly pig whose health began to wane.

Over time, specialties caused a noticeable shift in the Animals' priorities. At first, all the talk had been of the Colony's survival. Now, even as the Animals' individual talents began to emerge, they began to speak in terms of bettering themselves as individuals and families.

For most, these were signs that the Colony was maturing, its structure growing stronger and more sophisticated. But Gill and his closest friends noted the change with some alarm, as though the change signaled a greater selfishness or a weakened social bond.

Others feared that if some become too powerful, they could join together and destroy the competition that kept prices low and wages fair. To prevent this, the Colony voted to prohibit companies from growing too big and powerful, forming what Gander called "monopolies."

These measures aside, Animals would be allowed to prosper as far as smart decisions and hard work could carry them.


Time passed, and the Colony continued to thrive.

The Animals found that without humans constantly butchering the males while sparing the females for breeding purposes, they began to enjoy longer and more meaningful relationships. Soon, every Animal had found a mate to love and provide for. The family grew to form the basis of the Colony's whole society, the center around which everything revolved. It proved the ideal protector, provider and disciplinary authority for children, who now had a model for how they should act toward others.

The females, freed from the constant challenge of fending for themselves and their offspring without a caring mate, found time to beautify their homes and better nurture their children. The increased attention and instruction produced well-adjusted and polite youngsters who respected their elders and brought pride to their parents.

The families accepted responsibility for themselves and their neighbors. They worked hard, but also valued family time and leisure. While one mate worked, the other usually stayed home and joined neighbors in discussing important topics, gossiping a bit (or a lot), and keeping an eye on everyone's kids. With all these eyes constantly on them, the young ones found it hard to get away with bad behavior. Therefore, the only choice became wholesome activities. "Tag", "hide and seek," and various team games became popular.

The children found it fun to kick a large clump of wool and try to put it though a goal. At first, "hoofball" started as only a pickup activity to dissipate energy and get exercise, but it soon developed into something more. Players clearly gained exercise while learning life's lessons: learning to follow the referees' rules along with teamwork, sportsmanship and healthy competition. In the process, they discovered how to be either a good winner or good loser.

Parents joined together and formed schools which taught young ones Colony history, along with the skills needed for a successful life.

Through it all, one abiding realization seemed to throb in the Animals' minds like the charge from a lightning strike. *It's happening! It's actually working!*

Indeed, it truly seemed that Hoss' grand vision of freedom and liberty was actually coming to pass. To a bunch of escaped farm Animals, this outcome seemed too good and too fortunate to be true. And yet there it was: by simply following the old horse's good sense and courage, they seemed to have built their new Colony on a solid, workable foundation.

The colonists' numbers began to grow, and soon there arrived another unexpected blessing: the addition of new, previously unknown kinds of Animals to the colony.

First to come was a large bird, who landed with a great flourish of his brown wings in the compound's center one sunny morning.

"My name's Barnaby," he hooted loudly, "and my family and I are pure-blooded, North American horned owls. My family and I have been natives of this area for years. See, I've been watching you newcomers for many a day, and I'm starting to like what I'm seeing! You seem to be some of the wiser beasts I've spotted. So I'm wondering if—well, I guess what I'm asking is whether me and my family and friends could join you folks. These parts have been mighty quiet, even a bit forlorn since the folks who used to live here died off from that awful disease. We decided we could use the company."

The owl continued talking well into the day. While some were first inclined to consider him a nuisance, those who listened to him soon realized that he had much useful information to share. His knowledge of every inch, nook and cranny of their territory made him and his friends an invaluable new addition to the Colony.

An outbreak of pilfering led to the discovery of their second round of newcomers. Buster's cousin Tyler, one of the dogs who seemed to enjoy patrolling the compound's perimeter, one morning announced that someone seemed to be carrying off some of their best fallen timber during the night. Two days later, he walked in escorted by the proud culprits—a family of large brown rodents with broad flat tails, beady eyes and protruding front teeth.

*Beavers*, they called themselves. Their patriarch, a large quite fat specimen named Fergus, stood on his hind legs and fiercely proclaimed that all lumber within a hundred paces of flowing water was rightfully theirs, a claim they would proudly defend if put to it. Hoss wisely defused the confrontation by quickly granting their assertion, then followed up with an invitation to join the Colony and put their tree-cutting skills to even more profitable use. The beavers promptly accepted, and one of the Colony's most industrious species soon made its presence felt.

No one was happier about this development than Hoss, whose vision had included wild and newly freed Animals living in harmony.

One problem remained. Hoss soon realized that the dogs had been working hard without being compensated for their valuable service of patrolling Colony boundaries. He shared his concern with Gander, Gill, and Barnaby.

"You know," hooted Barnaby, "I noticed that the Indians used round stones and beads as tokens to bargain with and settle debts among themselves. They called it Wampum.

"Hey, that sounds like what we dug up that first day!" exclaimed Gander.

"So if someone does not have anything to trade," Hoss said, slowly understanding, "they could be given Wampum and beads in exchange. That way, we can all pitch in to pay the dogs, who can then use their beads and Wampum to buy food and necessities. "

"What about those of us whose skills aren't in... public demand?" asked Gill. "What am I supposed to do?"

Gander exchanged a helpless look with Hoss. It was, after all, one of their perennial issues—how to address the needs of a breed known for their intelligence and eloquence, but not for being useful in the barnyard.

It was then that Gander birthed an idea which, while a stroke of genius on the surface, would come to define the history of Animal Colony for years to come.

"Why don't you be our town crier? My father Samuel told me the most famous man in a human town was called a 'crier.' He stood in its center and called out the important news of the day in a loud voice every morning. That occupation sounds perfectly suited for you."

Gill clearly missed any potential slight in this recommendation, instead giving a look of pleased surprise and glancing around for the others' reactions.

"Indeed, that sounds perfectly suited for me," he snorted.

"Exactly," honked Gander.


The new ideas were duly presented and then voted in by an overwhelming majority of the Animals. And commerce, made more convenient by a form of currency, entered the life of the Colony.

As did public discourse, for Gill took to his new position with a flourish. The beavers carved out a stump in the center of the colony for Gill to stand on. Before long, the early morning gathering to hear Gill's news and exhortations for the day became a central and valued part of the Animals' routine.

And Gill rarely disappointed. At first, frigid temperatures not only kept the listeners shivering, but formed the backbone of his addresses. "This winter may be cold and hard," he said in his loudest voice, "but it is *our* winter. It is our own destinies we shape with these labors of ours."

The Animals appreciated Gill's speeches, for the heart of his message warmed their substance and soothed their labors. And Gill soon found a way to make his business work, by interjecting appeals for the other beasts' services into his speech. The featured Animals paid handsomely for these endorsements. Always, at the end of each speech, he dutifully recited the *Four Great Truths*.

Once again, the winter proved merciless. Despite their successful collaboration and the birth of commerce, the Animals suffered greatly through three withering blizzards that fell early in the new year.

The season had its casualties. Few of the young delivered during that miserable season survived. Four of the Colony's oldest citizens died in their sleep during the coldest of nights. Even Hoss had evenings during which he could not stop shivering, and the memory of those shroud-like waters seemed to afflict his thoughts and dreams to the point of death.

Eventually, however, the days seemed to grow longer and the winds to slowly grow warmer. Another spring was on its way. The plans each Animal had nurtured during the long evenings were now ripe to be put into action.

# Chapter Five

In this spirit of warmth and brotherhood, another spring came in earnest to the forest. And, in time, so did the occasion to plant another crop. Horses who had formed plowing and hauling enterprises used their brute strength to pull down and then haul away trees from a nearby plot of land which appeared proper ground for additional farmland.

When planting time came, the smaller Animals, namely the chickens, ducks and geese, were employed for their plucking and grain-handling abilities.

By the end of the spring, a plentiful crop had been planted. Those owning the fields then hired anyone willing to endure the heat of summer to pull the weeds which could threaten the harvest.

From the first appearance of green shoots, the corn's well-being became a point of sheer exuberance among those who had planted it. Competition for the cleanest field kept many of those farming busy pulling weeds from sunrise to sunset. Indeed, hard work became a symbol of all that had gone right since arriving at Animal Colony.

Somehow, of all the Colony's achievements thus far—reclaiming a dead and abandoned Indian village, the establishment of a free economy—nothing seemed to gladden the hearts of the Animals like the sight of their cornfields growing taller by the day.

Once again, the sight of mature corn led some Animals to call for a feast day, causing Hoss' penchant for caution to reassert itself.

"We have no idea how long this bountiful weather will last," he announced. "Wouldn't we be far wiser to consume this blessing in gratitude and conservation, rather than be caught by surprise by some future calamity?"

This time, however, Gander urged Hoss to relent in his approach, since the grain had been donated from the surplus by willing farmers. It was a good time to encourage the Colony in celebrating and expressing gratitude to their Creator.

So, on a crisp day in the early fall, the Animals spread out a blanket of fresh pine needles and bark across the open heart of the Colony grounds, then treated themselves to a heaping mound of freshly harvested ears of corn. All the Animals were represented, even the dogs, who left a token scout force in the unlikely event of attack.

Once again, Hoss looked out over the bunch from his seat of honor at the thickest part of the seed mound, and remarked to himself what a good-natured and congenial bunch of Animals they were.

The festivities that followed only confirmed that impression. After eating came songs of freedom and commemorative dances by the little ones. The dogs attempted a display of precision stalking to show off their military and scouting skills. However, the perfect formation was broken when the lead hound spotted a blue-jay stealing some of the food nearby and streaked away, barking ferociously. One precocious piglet stood up and recited an ode to the heroes of the Great River Crossing, mistakenly labeling it "the Big Water Passing" and earning for himself an unusually loud chorus of laughter and applause. Representatives from each of the Colony species came forward to offer prayers of gratitude to the Creator, as well as expressions of honor and respect to Hoss.

Barnaby the Owl stepped forward to once again express his gratitude at being admitted into the Colony, launching yet another interminable speech. Of course, the Animals were far too kind and courteous to forcibly stop the marathon, so the ordeal only ended when one of the chickens, trying in vain to "hold it in," accidentally laid an egg which then rolled through the audience, clearing a broad path of squawking and laughing listeners.

In all, the day proved an equal mix of pomp and comedy, which was perfect for everyone's taste.

It was a glorious year, one which would long be remembered as among "the best of times" in Animal Colony's history. Food was plentiful, security reigned, and the blessings of liberty seemed to resonate in the hearts of all. The once-dead Indian village now bustled with activity, laughter, and the beauty of happy families. The Colony's youngsters roamed the forest under the watchful eye of their parents and canine protectors, exploring a vast new playground of deep forest glades, sparkling streams and even several ponds courtesy of their new beaver friends.

If the blessings of the earlier crop success were indeed dissipated in the throes of apparent good fortune, no one seemed inclined to spoil the good moods long enough to urge restraint. For in fact, this golden life, enjoying the fruits of honest labor, seemed exactly the fulfillment of Hoss' long-ago vision—an earthly paradise of unbridled freedom, enjoyment, hard work, and plenty.


In late afternoon on one of the fall season's truly mild days, the dogs' frantic barking roused the Colony from its usual midday stupor. The beasts came bounding into the compound's center with a speed and recklessness they had never dared before. Within seconds, several disapproving parents had gathered to scold the over-exuberant hounds.

That is, until the dogs started to explain themselves.

As it turned out, a routine patrol along the river shore had revealed something terrifying. Their eyes had clearly made out two settlers hunting on the opposite shore. The dogs had asked their friend Barnaby, the Owl to investigate and he had confirmed their worst fears. The men were armed with muskets. Worse still, the men had seen the Colony's cows grazing. After spotting the free Animals, the men had hurriedly gathered, talked for some time, then headed back the way they had come.

The listening Animals gasped in surprise and fear. Clearly, an attack was imminent. Immediately, frightened glances turned to Hoss for reassurance and direction.

"Surely they mean to return and enslave us again." he mused. "Thanks to the early warning you dogs have given us, we have some time to prepare. So let us be ready to greet our invaders with a welcome they will never forget!"

"Wait a minute," said Gill's brother Norm. "We came here to save our lives, because you warned that many of us would not live out the winter. So what is the gain in dying here just to avoid being taken back?"

Gill, foreseeing the collapse of his morning's talk, immediately shared his dim view. Surely, the whole matter was little more than another overheated canine distraction. "We don't need to live in fear," he called out. "The settlers are reasonable folk, just like us. Surely they will see what a civilized place we have carved out for ourselves, be duly impressed, wish us well and be on their way."

At this, Henry the goose launched himself to the speaker's stump with a sudden flurry of his wings. "I don't know about anyone else," he honked in a determined voice, "but to me, freedom is about much more than survival. One minute of the liberty we've enjoyed is worth more to me than ten years under the yoke of slavery to humans. To preserve that freedom, I would gladly give my very life!"

The passion and conviction in Henry's voice wrenched an instant shout of agreement from everyone listening. The whole compound rang with the echoes of their acclamation, and just that quickly, the matter was settled.

The Colony would fight to the last beast.

The Animals threw themselves into the task of preparation. First, the Colony's wisest gathered for an hour-long strategy meeting during which a cunning military plan was devised. During and after the council, the other beasts busied themselves gathering stones, digging pits and providing hiding places for the young. The dogs suggested that, instead of simply patrolling the Colony's perimeters, they take up positions even beyond them, deep in the woods, in order to give more warning when the attack came.

Gill lamented the fact that muskets gave the settlers an overwhelming advantage of superior firepower. Hoss countered that after they fired their muskets, there came a moment of opportunity during the pause to reload.

Eventually, it was agreed that the watchdogs would bark once if the settlers had crossed the water upstream and would be attacking over land. If they were coming by boat straight at the Colony, the dogs would bark twice. Then, the Animals' sophisticated battle plan would swing into action.

Three days passed before the preparations were complete. At last, the Colony settled into an uneasy and deceptive calm.

About five days later, the dreaded two barks echoed over the treetops, emphatic and unmistakable. For a second, the entire population seemed to freeze in place.

Then, with hardly a look at the others, everyone scurried around to their assigned positions. The children and their mothers hid in their homes, in the woods, in ravines, or in the pits. The horses, dogs and other warriors positioned themselves in their pre-arranged hiding places where they could wait for their opportunity to ambush the settlers.

Chester the goose and a half-dozen others of the Colony's bravest waited at the far side of the Colony's perimeter, much more loosely concealed. They had volunteered to draw fire.

Chester watched as, in the distance through the trees, the settlers paddled their boats ashore and grouped near Freedom Rock.

Everything now fell deathly quiet.

Both the invading men and the Colony's defenders hardly dared breathe. After what felt like an hour, the light-footed settlers tiptoed into the Colony itself. Holding bridles and ropes as well as torches and the anticipated muskets, the men seemed to think they had entered nothing more than a deserted Indian village. That is, until one of them, looking down at his feet, silently motioned for the others to examine the ground.

It was riddled with hundreds of fresh Animal footprints.

Then Chester gasped so strongly that he feared he had been heard. First one, then a second settler did something unexpected: they threw their torches onto shelter roofs. He fought the impulse to call out a warning—*there were Animals hiding in those structures!*

As the leader of their very first maneuver, Chester knew the decision was his. He instantly realized that if he waited for the settlers to reach the intended spot in the village center, Animals trapped in burning homes would not have time to escape.

He had to act, and he had to act fast.

With a loud honk that hardly sounded like that of a goose, Chester jumped out into the path of the settlers and, flapping his wings wildly, charged the men headfirst. Confused and surprised, several of them fired their muskets and the air seemed torn apart by loud reports and billowing smoke.

Chester suddenly cried out again, only in pain. One of the bullets had struck him and shattered the bone of his outstretched wing.

Luckily, Chester's fellow volunteer decoys did not remain hidden, despite the peril. Gander and a motley assortment of barnyard beasts bolted from their cover and ran bravely into the fray. Gander actually found his bad leg a fighting advantage, as his uneven gait made him a poor target for enemy shooters. A furious volley of musket shots rang out, and the air now filled with screams of the injured and dying.

Then, a blessed pause came. The one-shot muskets had spent their bullets, and the remaining defenders now had their chance.

With a terrifying blend of wild whinnying, bellowed lowing and enraged barking, dogs and horses and cattle made their charges from their hiding places on every side of the hapless men. The beasts reached the human cordon and launched themselves upon it with lifted hoof and bared teeth. Hoss reared back on rippling haunches and leveled a withering swipe of his hooves across the human position. There came a loud crunch and one of the men fell limp, felled by the blow.

The chaos redoubled as mothers and children now began to run, heedless and screaming, from their burning homes. Some of them, panicked more by fire than the actual combat, actually collided with the men trying to shake off biting dogs and trampling horses.

One man was already down and another joined him on the ground, overwhelmed by the onslaught. The others glanced at the frightful sight, took in what was happening and desperately gathered the fallen in shaky arms.

In a moment, the human resolve was broken. The remaining men turned back toward the forest and ran, shouting in rage, for their very lives. Still pursued by dogs and horses, they sprinted through the trees with loud, hoarse shouts. When they reached the shore, they did not pause but jumped into their canoes and began rowing wildly onto the water. A single musket shot, fired more in spiteful revenge than careful aim, was their last retort.

The Animals had defeated their former captors.

*Victory was theirs!*

A great cry rose through the forest as the awesome realization swept through the victorious Animals.

However, the victory had exacted a tragic toll. Unfortunately, Chester's premature charge had resulted in higher-than-anticipated casualties. His early call to battle had forced them to charge from farther away than intended, compromising their ambush and giving several settlers the opportunity to reload and fire. As a result, several of the colony's fighters had been killed or wounded. Buster was severely injured, bearing a vicious tear along his throat. A teenaged ram, one horse and two dogs lay bloodied and still in the dirt. Cotton, an ironically named member of the cow family, suffered a badly mangled leg.

Grief proved the prevailing emotion for the first half-hour following battle's end. Barnaby, the owl, who had gained a working knowledge of medical care from observing the Indians, used special leaves to bandage up the wounded. A somber detail carted away the bodies in anticipation of later burial.

But ultimately, the grimness of the battle also ended up heightening the victors' sense of elation. After the initial shock had faded, the assembled beasts of Animal Colony marched in circles at the village's center, lofting great shouts of triumph and pumping their limbs and wings defiantly into the sky.

At last, Hoss managed to calm the impromptu war dance to utter a few sentiments.

"Do you realize, my fellow Animals, that we can now truly call ourselves free in the deepest of ways? Our former enslavers tried to reclaim us, and we defeated them! We have earned our liberty once and for all. We had made a down payment with our sweat and toil, but now we have paid it off. Animal Colony can no longer be accused of being just a band of runaway farm Animals waiting to be rounded up and driven back to our pens. Our freedom has not been free. It has now been bought by those who have fought and gave their lives!"

At first, the speech was greeted by silence and stares. Hoss hesitated momentarily, wondering if his improvised remarks had inadvertently offended someone. But he soon realized that the hush was merely his fellow Animals' amazement at his burst of eloquence. An instant later, they all began to cheer even louder and more emphatically than before.

Gander stepped up beside him.

"Sorry to bring the mood back down to details," the goose cautioned, "but I think we must take measures to ensure that they do not return. We must guarantee that if they do, the humans will meet an even stronger, more organized and better prepared defense force than the first time."

A long and fierce debate ensued. It ended with general agreement that despite their sheer and complete liberty, the Animals needed to form some kind of central authority to coordinate essential matters like providing for their common defense.

Soon, its establishment narrowed down to the appointment of a single leader for Animal Colony. Someone whose fairness and wisdom was implicitly trusted by all. An Animal who could protect their rights of life, liberty and the pursuit of happiness, even as they governed according to the *Great Truths*. Nobody wanted a leader capable of gaining too much power over his fellow beasts, so an additional wrinkle was added: each sector would reserve the right to elect leaders to handle issues within their territory and send representatives to a Central Council. The Central Council would meet with the Leader every month to advise him on key decisions involving Colony border protection and any disagreements between the Sectors. All other issues were the Sectors' sole responsibility.

In the wake of the days' heroics, several names emerged for the office of Leader, like Buster, Gill and Hoss. But within a few long harangues on various candidates' behalf, and speeches praising their respective achievements, it quickly became clear. The truly pioneering and beloved leader among them was the one who had borne the vision for Animal Colony's birth.

And so Hoss became the first Official Leader of Animal Colony. The vote was met with long cheers and even longer periods of embarrassed silence as Hoss struggled to gain control of his emotions.

That is how, all within the span of a single day, Animal Colony weathered its first hostile military action, won its freedom, established a central government, and voted itself an official Leader.

However, for the Animals who accomplished all this, these milestones paled in emotional importance next to the sheer thrill of having won real independence.

For some of them, liberty had been something of an abstraction until their actual defeat of the humans. Many had joined the escape out of vague ties of loyalty and kinship rather than a keen understanding of liberty and self-determination. For them, the main difference between Animal Colony and the Masters' settlement had been the simple absence of human beings.

Now, it truly sank in for everyone that they were their own rulers. A sense of elation and celebration hovered over the Colony for days after the village's damage had been repaired and their dead buried.

Even the humble chickens and ducks seemed to hold their heads higher as they went about their business. Hoss even noticed that their traditional neck-jerk motions seemed to grow more pronounced—as though the birds were actually beginning to strut from sheer self-pride.

The dogs now carried themselves like grizzled veterans, adopting dramatic poses of vigilance at every opportunity––unaware of how silly they often looked. Buster, Hoss and his fellow horses were treated with respect and awe.

Most heartwarming of all, however, was the sense of unity and harmony which seemed to settle over the Colony in the months that followed. Despite the obvious differences in their sizes, aptitudes and needs, the Colony's diverse species began to feel like true members of an extended family. The usual inter-species squabbling which had always dominated their old barnyard died down. The dogs cut way down on their perverse pastime of chasing the chickens. They even refrained from shaking rainwater out of their fur in the immediate vicinity of others.

Animal Colony was expanding in both numbers and territory. Those moving to the new areas developed the land, organized and sent representatives to the Central Council. Competition between the Sectors kept revenues and services in balance. In a similar way, competition between businesses kept prices and wages reasonable. Animals with their own enterprises actually found it necessary to compete for employees by offering better pay and benefits.

As a result, prosperity became the rule for the next several years.

# Chapter Six

Several winters later, a half-dozen of the beavers were seen cutting down trees not far from the closest stream. Soon, Champ and Suzie trotted into the compound, pulling those same logs. Over the next several days, his horse family labored unceasingly to lash the beams upon their existing hut, creating a structure which effectively doubled its size.

With some of the leftover Wampum Champ had earned through several years of hard labor, he paid the beavers to find several dozen choice flat stones from the creek bottom. He then laid down a new floor for the entrance of his home. Working day after day, he hauled bark and wood from fallen trees to cover the expansion. Other Animals came and went, adding their respective talents to the overhaul of Champ's residence. Soon, the structure was by far the largest in all of Animal Colony.

Some of the others, still in the midst of their winters' idleness, grumbled at the size of Champ's expansion. They feared he might be taking advantage of his new prosperity, not to mention his relationship to Hoss, to build himself an arrogant display of power over his fellow citizens.

But Gander and others pointed out that Champ and the other horses were by far the largest of the Colony's beasts, and several years of foaling had left their families too large for their current homes. They had all seen Hoss and the oldest horses sleep on piles of hay which had been patiently gathered and pushed against the outer walls of their shelters. Clearly, the expansion had been motivated by urgent necessity, not greed or pride.

"Besides," Gander continued. "Our leader's brother paid for the expansion with Wampum won of his own labors. This was merely another blessing given him by the wonderful new life we all now share! The expansion had created jobs for others. Indeed, we all have the right to work harder and longer to pay for the things our families want and need most! Isn't that the glory of our newfound liberty?"

Gander's arguments won the day. Before long, other hard-working and enterprising Animals began to spend their extra Wampum and beads on items for their families. Some began to pay Animals more skilled than them to perform tasks they found difficult, like gathering food, or fresh straw for their roosts. Others saved their beads against the potential of another hard winter. Still others spent their wealth freely during the fall's feasting.

This air of relative plenty did not mean, however, that the Animals had forgotten their previous spirit of helpfulness and compassion. Halfway through the season, the dwelling place of Bruce the bull and his family was struck by lightning during an evening thunderstorm. It burst into flame and burned to the ground.

His mate Margie and her calf, who were enjoying one of the most carefree and memorable times of their lives, were now heartbroken. But the very next morning, the entire Colony threw itself into action at Hoss' urging. As though it was yet another summer lark, a large and joyous crowd set about building for their brother an entirely new, larger and altogether more preferable dwelling place.

As always, Hoss led the way, hauling the frame timber well into the following night. Before three days had passed, the cows were gratefully settled into a cleaner, warmer and more spacious shelter then they had ever known.

The case of the cows was far from exceptional. Several mishaps befell other assorted members of the Colony that summer. Each was quickly dispatched in a spirit of brotherhood, joyous compassion and freewill. When the individual was not able to handle a crisis themselves, their extended family stepped in. If that was not enough, friends stepped up. If more help was needed, charitable groups mustered aid.

Hoss never forgot the frustration he had felt trying to solve everyone's problems by himself during Animal Colony's first year. Solving one crisis seemed to simply cause others to spring up in their place. His solution now was to stay out of the way and encourage Animals to solve their own problems with innovation, extra effort, and mutual help.

This policy was severely challenged when, on one of the stifling days of early summer the following year, a bank of grey, black-tipped clouds massed upon the western horizon. Soon, cool raindrops began to fall. Accustomed to the usual barnyard thinking, the Animals looked up and smiled in gratitude.

Rain, of course, brings plenty—every good beast knows that.

When the drops thickened into a deafening downpour, the smarter mothers nosed their young ones outside for a spur-of-the-moment, trouble-free bath. Their intentions were soon thwarted as some of the more rambunctious adolescents began sliding on their bellies down the Colony's muddy inclines, covering themselves in grime and leaves.

Thankfully, the rain lasted while the mothers rushed out to punish their wayward ones, drenching themselves in the process. Soon, both youngsters and parents were joining in the fun.

By day's end, young and old had enjoyed hours of raucous fun and received a good bath in the process.

But the rain did not end at sunset.

It did not end at sunrise, either.

By noon the following day, those living by the river stood knee-deep in water creeping into their dwellings. Within hours, what had begun as a blessing, then soured into a mere annoyance, had deepened into an emergency.

Shortly before sunset, a rumble was heard at the Colony's western edge. Those who peered into the trees saw a sudden darkness overwhelm the forest. One minute later, a brown wall roared through the River Sector, sweeping away trees, homes and Animals alike.

Several new dwellings, especially those near the fork of the river where many pigs and chicken lived, were destroyed. And tragically, three young lambs and dozens of non-swimmers were found drowned in clumps of bushes, trees—or never found at all.

The tragedy was devastating. Nearly a third of Animal Colony was directly affected through loss of life, loss of home, loss of job or loss of sustenance. The desolation continued; floodwaters remained high for more than a week.

Hoss felt his heart wrench at the sight of Animals wading through the mud and muck, trying to salvage what they could of their possessions. Those who had lost loved ones stood staring into space, muted by grief.

As leader, Hoss knew that he had to step forward with encouragement and a plea for mutual cooperation. He sent out the word that every Animal should come to the speaker's stump for his address.

"My fellow colonists," he started, "we weathered being starved under the tyranny of the settlers. We survived the terror of the river crossing. We defeated the settlers' attack on our freedom. Just as we've made it through every other seemingly impossible situation, we will make it through this tragedy. We will do it by working together and helping each other. We arc all brothers and sisters. We are family—and families take care of each other."

"Therefore, I encourage each of you to share with those affected by the flood. If any Animal needs food, please feed them. If they need shelter, please take them in. If they need work, I hope you'll help them find jobs. Let's get to work and do whatever it takes. But I encourage caution for those wanting to rebuild in the flooded area, as this may happen again. You have the freedom to do so, but I urge you to use the low land for crops. Not for homes."

Many, if not most, took up Hoss' challenge and helped their fellow colonists. They soon had an abundance of donated food, household goods and volunteers. The sheer volume forced them to form charitable groups to organize the work and distribute the resources. Some groups set up feeding stations where those working could conveniently eat and not have to trudge long distances for food. Some took leave from their normal labor to volunteer time. Others offered to watch children while the parents went to help.

Many inter-species friendships were fostered during this time, contributing to an overall sense that in some ways, the flood had turned into a sort of blessing.

By the fall of that year, everything was as close to normal as possible. However, the loss of a third of that year's harvest caused an economic slump that affected everyone, not only those who had lived close to the river.

Because of the downturn, Gill began to grumble, quietly and out of Hoss' earshot at first. He complained that the Colony was in danger of turning into a playground for those blessed with the right kinds of talents.

His speaking out began slowly and modestly, only expressed in idle conversation. Soon, those who routinely gathered to hear his morning reports began to notice a certain acid tone and critical bent to his words. Then, gathering small groups from among the Colony's less prosperous Animals, he began to suggest that injustice might be creeping into their once equal and even-handed season of plenty.

The next winter proved abnormally dry and mild, and Gill began to grumble a bit more. His fellow pigs' rooting now yielded nothing, as the unusually packed soil refused to open under their hardest efforts. The beavers complained that surrounding creek banks were "pulling up short," in their own peculiar lingo, but few quite understood the rodents' meaning.

In fact, water levels were dropping quickly. The river was becoming brackish and too shallow for growth.

Meanwhile, the Colony's young ones, eager to enjoy the outdoors as soon as possible, were the first to report that the forest's flowers had failed to bloom on time. By the time the forest plants had produced anemic brown buds in place of leaves, everybody knew something was wrong.

When Hoss attempted to break ground on his spring planting, the splintered branch he used for plowing broke. He first blamed the problem on old wood, and the beavers hastily gnawed a fresher implement. It fared no better. For hours, the old horse labored to dig a single row. After half a day, all he had accomplished was a paltry little furrow, shallow and crumbling off in a dry breeze.

As a result, they realized the somber truth. They had entered a full-scale drought before anybody had thought to even bring up the word. In fact, the idea was not even broached until most of their spring crop had failed entirely.

Finally, alarmed by the lack of success in the fields, Hoss called a meeting in his brother's new dwelling place, out of the withering sun.

"Nice big place for a gathering," Gill muttered under his breath, his observation intended for several of his most disgruntled supporters milling nearby.

Gander, however, was waddling past and overheard the remark. Leaning over, he retorted, "Did you notice it's no fancier than many others, only bigger? And if you wonder why the size, did you see all the other horses standing outside? With all of us in here, there's not even room for their own family!"

The goose continued on, too quickly to see Gill make eye contact with his friends and exchange a smirk.

"My brothers and sisters," Hoss began at last with a smile of deep satisfaction, "we have had some wonderful years, and an even more blessed last winter. I have laid before you a vision of blessed liberty and plenty, and I have taken as deep a pleasure in seeing it come to pass as anyone."

A few cheers went up at that, but they were halting and tentative. No one was quite sure if Hoss had summoned them to celebrate their recent past or some other, more disruptive purpose.

"However, I have to confess that today finds me a bit alarmed. Our planting season has not gone well. Another winter will soon be here. It promises to be just as merciless as many before. Can anyone tell me that they have saved enough corn to eat this winter?"

He was greeted by a heavy silence as most gazes fell. The pause felt so solemn that it provoked Hoss to an even graver question.

"How many of you will have enough seed corn to plant next season?"

A pathetic scattering of paws, hooves and wings lifted in the air. Gander lifted his wing the highest and glanced about himself in alarm.

"Oh, my goodness. We may be in trouble if we have another dry year. Have any of you prepared for *that*?"

A dozen of the Animals did not hear the end of Hoss' sentence. A line of scowling beasts had begun to head out the door.

As Hoss had reluctantly predicted, the winter was as bitter as any they could remember. Wave after wave of glacial temperatures and unforgiving winds swept across the Colony's territory. By that time, hunger had already gripped many of the Animals in its cruel jaws.

The joys of summer past were quickly forgotten in the wake of long, frigid nights and the constant gnawing of empty stomachs. Within weeks, hunger had brought with it illness and malnutrition. Then children began to die.

Many of the Animals took the less fortunate into their homes and shared their food with both other families and other species. Gander especially pushed his reserves to the limit, but he determined to save a bag of seed no one could touch, even to the point of death. Generalized despair might prevail, but he, like some others, still had faith in the future of Animal Colony.

None of the Animal families were struck by the famine's savagery any more tragically than the hogs'. Already, their lack of practical gifts had shut them out from a great deal of the general prosperity. Now, with their plight worsened by a summer of exuberant partying, they were the first to complain. (Some argued that since the hogs were already roundly fat to begin with, they were doubly disposed to feel hunger, and triply disposed to complain loudly about its effects. That argument did little to create harmony and goodwill.) Nevertheless, by mid-winter, the pigs presented a heart-wrenching picture of the Colony's overall deterioration.

"We're facing an outright famine," Hoss declared somberly during another evening gathering. "Maybe even worse than anything we faced with our masters. But tonight, we're all on our own, with no humans to even pretend to intervene."

"There *is* food in the Colony," Gill retorted. "Except it's not being shared."

"Where is that?" asked Jada the duck. The sharpness in her voice and a fierce gleam in her eyes betrayed what most of the others knew. The Colony's fowl population, chickens and geese and ducks, were also suffering keenly from the lack of food. In past months, they had been among the first to lose their foraged food supply. The creeks and ponds had failed to offer green shoots and succulents when the creekbeds had dried up. Those seeking a drink now had to travel a fair distance to the main riverbanks.

"Some of us Animals," Gill said, shifting his eyes grimly from side to side, "profited more than others when times were good. Many have hoarded large stashes of grain and foodstuffs not even a stone's throw away from their hungry brethren."

"But those are the careful savings of those who heeded my warnings!" interrupted Hoss with an outraged snort. "There's nothing sinister about that. Those are badly needed reserves for winter use and spring planting! They were merely being prudent!"

"How do you define prudent, dear respected leader? Having more than everybody else? Having a full stomach when others around you are going hungry?"

"But that is why I tried to urge caution months ago!" replied Hoss. Frustration clearly showed in the backwards angle of his long ears and the fire in his large eyes. "I warned that those who did not heed my warnings would place their lives at risk. Suffering the consequences of your own folly does not mean that your more careful brothers are to blame!"

But somehow, the mood among the large crowd of hungry Animals seemed to turn against the beloved leader. Gazes turned dark and angry. A low rumble of disapproval began to flow from beaks throughout the crowd.

"And yet the result is that many are left to go without," Gill thundered, "while others have more than enough! Not everyone has listened to their charitable impulse! Not everyone is pitching in to help their neighbors!"

"It's harder to do, with no relief in sight," said Gander. "Fixing a flooded or demolished home is one thing when most homes are intact. But now, we're all facing the famine, and no one knows when there will be food again, if ever!"

"All I know is, some of us have, and some of us haven't!" Gill's brother Norm shouted, raising his snout in exasperation.

"Now wait a minute," broke in Kelynn, the young bull. "I do remember Hoss spoiling our fun by begging us to be careful with our summer leftovers."

"Yes, but he certainly joined in all the fun after we'd gone ahead and ignored his warnings, didn't he?" asked Gill. "You know that I love and revere Hoss as much or more than any of you. But I'm having trouble reconciling our leader's talk with some of his actions. After all, who's the one now with all the grain and a considerable amount of Wampum?"

No one raised a limb in reply.

"And weren't freedom and prosperity supposed to work for everyone? I don't know about you, but I look around and I see only a part of the Colony truly living a dream life.

The rest of us are having to sweat the months ahead, with no one to fend for us but ourselves."

"But isn't that the point?" interrupted Kelynn. "Didn't escaping the settlers and risking everything for liberty mean the freedom to fend for ourselves?"

Gill turned towards the young bull and fixed him with a hateful glare. "Kelynn, eight months ago you were pulling your mother's milk, hardly able to walk straight. What in the world would you know about fending for yourself?"

Kelynn looked around and, realizing that no argument would be lifted in his defense, hung his head and slunk away.

Hoss lowered his gaze and spoke in a low voice, intended for Gill rather than the mob beside him.

"You've accused me of reaching prosperity," Hoss said steadily, "by stealing from the Colony and abusing my power. That's a cruel lie which I absolutely deny."

"You got us here under false pretenses!" shouted Gill, his anger unsubsided. "You painted a picture of plenty, of comfort, of ease. And today, you and your friends seem to be the only ones tasting of it! And worse yet, you seem to suggest that we victims of this drought are at fault for our misfortune. Well, I say, where there are victims, there are surely victimizers! Look around, my hungry friends, and remember those standing with full bellies and no wish to offer a share to their fellow beast!"

The meeting ended on that sour note. However, a mere two days later—without even a word to Hoss, Gander or any of the Colony's harder working citizens—the rest of the Animals planned and convened a vote in the compound's central space.

It was a cold assembly but given its agenda, this group was not about to gather in Champ's living room again. This time, Hoss' family was not among the invited guests.

Besides, Gill's speaking skills were in top form.

"My fellow Animals, the great experiment in liberty which is Animal Colony today stands in need of a sharp readjustment. We are grateful to no longer be slaves of our human oppressors. We are heartened to stand in charge of our own destinies for the first time in Animal memory. However, the promise of that first grand vision which inspired us to take that fateful walk out of the Master's clutches has not paid off for all of us. Today, many of us are suffering. Our mothers are grieving, and bellies are empty, even as scores of our neighbors sit back enjoying a time of ease. That is wrong! It is unjust! Were we not told that we all had rights? Were we not told that we each had the right to achieve comfort and prosperity in this new cradle of freedom? I say to each of you who has been forced to endure this suffering, this indignity—you are not the beneficiaries of that once-great vision, you are its *victims*!"

Cheers filled the air, loud and fierce, mixed in with growls and shouted slogans. "We demand fairness! We demand fairness!"

"Well today, my fellow Animals, I say it is time to make the promise of this noble Colony available to all. It is time to spread the wealth."

A thick row of beasts immediately raised a lusty cheer upon Gill's well-timed pause.

"Tonight's victims need a champion, and that champion will never come from within the ranks of the Victimizers. It must come from the untried ranks of those who share your pain, your anguish, your hunger! That is why first of all, with all due affection and honor to Hoss our cherished first chief, I offer that we need to elect new leadership. We need to progress with a fresh vision and new ideas, to take Animal Colony the rest of the way to true justice and fairness. We need change we can believe in!"

There was a brief pause. Everyone turned and saw that Hoss and his friends had joined them, drawn by the ruckus.

Everyone expected Hoss to say something, but he did not move. In fact, no one had ever seen him more perfectly still than at that moment.

"If you elect me Leader," Gill continued, his voice lofting into a higher pitch, "I will immediately begin the Sharing, an emergency program of pooling our resources into one common fund. Let all of us, according to his treasures, based on his wealth, give a small portion so that others may live. We must give liberally, so the promise can live on for every family and every young one! When that is done, I will immediately begin to redistribute the Sharing based on need, starting with the most humble and destitute and on to the most esteemed of the Colony. Never again will a mother have to grieve a starving child! Never again will a surviving youngster have to go hungry at night! And when the crisis is over, of course, we can end the Sharing, and go back to the way things were."

The crescendo which greeted this point almost resembled another installment of the summer feast. Only a few, plaintive voices of opposition were drowned out by the cacophony of whistles and cheers.

Hoss shook his head and neighed in frustration. "I'm all for Animals volunteering to help others," he said. "In fact, I've been planning to call for another time of mutual aid, just as I have always done in times of crisis. I'm only against taking each other's savings by force. Let's have another time of voluntary sharing, and perhaps those of us with more in reserve need to dig deeper than before. But we can do this without seizing each other's property. What's wrong with simply opening our hearts and our stores out of our own free will?"

"Because no one is doing enough, that's why!" shouted Gill. "You pledge to propose another voluntary sharing, but the subject seems to have only come up when the hungry folks raised their voice. The time is past! You and your wealthy friends have sat in comfort while your fellow beasts suffered and their babies died, and you didn't do enough!"

Suddenly, a chorus of angry voices rose up against Gill.

"That's not true!" hooted Barnaby, the owl. "I've been taking food to my neighbors for weeks now!"

Gander added his response. "My whole family has been feeding five others without ever telling a soul! Besides, spring is just around the corner."

Hoss looked around in amazement. It seemed that dozens of the families who had listened to him the most, and who today had the deepest food savings, had without calling attention to themselves been quietly engaged in charitable acts.

Gill, however, was not swayed.

"The fact remains that large numbers of us are going without!" he thundered. "There are huge inequities between the rich and the poor! And if the promise of Animal Colony is to be fulfilled, that must end today!"

Hoss raised his head once more and sighed so heavily that it was heard nearly to the back row.

"I still think the older way is best," he replied. "However, if a majority of you think this emergency measure is necessary, and if it will end when it is no longer needed, I will abide by your decision. I was ready to step down, anyway. Four years is long enough to be in office. Public service should be about taking your turn, not about getting re-elected or staying a leader forever. I am now ready to get back to the real world of productive endeavors. I believe I did my best, and served well."

With that, Hoss bowed his head low to the ground, turned around and walked away in silence.

The actual vote took place several minutes later.

Gill was indeed elected to replace Hoss as leader of Animal Colony, and the Great Readjustment was put into action even before the sun set.

It was agreed that the burdensome task of gathering and counting the results of the Sharing would fall upon Gill himself. He, after all, was adept at numbers and things of the mind—though little else.

"One more thing," Gill said softly as the meeting began to dwindle to its end. "In return for my services, I ask you to let me keep a modest additional portion, beyond the Share my starving family receives, as a fair and just compensation for my work and for those who will be helping me."

The assembly was tired and restless, and so his request was granted by simple acclamation.

Nobody, in their haste, thought to ask the size of the share Gill proposed to keep for himself.

# Chapter Seven

The next morning dawned with the sound of growling. Remembering that the dogs now carried out the vital function of protecting the Colony from outside enemies, nearly every head of household came storming from his front door, ready for a mortal threat.

It turned out the noise did not come from outside the compound or even out of doors at all. It had come from within the hut of Bruce, the cow.

"What are you dogs doing?" asked Bruce plaintively. Only a few feet away, the hounds were rummaging with their long noses through his food supplies.

"Collecting the Sharing," announced Bernard. "Do you not remember last night's election? We're here to take a share of the wealth the fortunates have accumulated and share it with those less fortunate!"

"I'm not fortunate," said Bruce, "just hard-working! Besides, we're not wealthy. We just heeded Leader Hoss' warning to set something aside for a day like this one!"

"Besides, this feels more like confiscation!" mooed Marge, his mate. "Couldn't we just take what we feel is fair and bring it to the reserve?"

"It is not your place to decide your fair Share," said Bernard. "Brother Gill has wisely estimated each lodge's rightful contribution, and asked us to come collect it. It is the only way to make sure nobody holds back."

"But I was quite willing to Share," said Bruce. "I had already planned to bring in something later this morning."

"Well, then," Bernard said with a cool grin, "consider this a helpful service call."

The air of consternation spread over the Colony that whole day and the next, as dogs made the rounds of each family's lodgings. One by one they took away basketfuls of grain and food far larger than what most had imagined would be called for. Cries of, "that's for my spring planting!" and "what will I use now to trade for a new plow?" rang out across the dwellings.

Gill showed up later than usual for his announcement as town crier that day. When he did, he faced an unusually large and stirred up crowd. Another, red-faced pig stood behind him.

"Because of the great task you have asked me to perform, my fellow Animals," he said in his most official voice, "I have decided with great reluctance that I cannot continue in my beloved role as your town crier. Perhaps someday, when equality and justice is restored to the Colony, I will have the privilege of resuming those pleasurable duties once more. However, for now, the hard labor of gathering and administering the Sharing of our

Colony's common goods is almost more than I can handle. Therefore, I have appointed my brother Norm to serve in my place. Norm is also gifted in public speaking and reporting. However, I will remain in close contact with him, so you may know that when Norm speaks, his words have Gill the pig's seal of approval."

With that, Gill stepped and shuffled off towards the great pit where the Sharing was being weighed out and stored.

A few weeks later, with the temperature warming and signs of spring appearing everywhere, the Animals awoke to the sounds of rain pattering on their bark rooftops.

Hoss awoke first, then eagerly woke up his two sons, Jaxon and Jevin.

"Dad, can't you sleep in for once?" grumbled Jaxon, his oldest and most spirited. "After all, they've chosen another leader. If you work hard, they'll just say more nasty things about you!"

"Being leader was never the prize," Hoss countered. "What mattered to me was a chance to steer the Colony in the right direction."

"But what about being accused of not caring?" asked Jevin. "Of being unfair?"

"I have to admit, that does stick in my jaw. But let's not sit here neighing about it. Those raindrops mean the soil will have moisture, at least for a little while. And we have food to replace," said their father. "Let's go back to work."

"But they'll just come and take it again!" whined Jevin. "What's the use?"

"No, that was just an emergency measure," Hoss replied. "They'll repeal it as soon as they're sure the drought is over and everyone has been taken care of. Besides: I'm not against the Sharing. If that's the best way to temporarily help our fellow Animals, then I accept it. So let's go!"

Bedraggled, the horses lumbered to their feet and left the warmth of their home. Outside, however, they found a surprise. It seems many other colonists had been struck with the same idea, for two cow families and Gander's entire clan were walking on their way to their fields.

"Off to work!" bellowed one bull. "The cupboards are bare again!"

"At least there's rain in the air," Gander said with a nod. "It's a good day to start the work of stocking back up!"

On the way past the compound's center, Norm was giving the morning report.

"According to our great leader Gill," he bellowed, "the task of administering the great Sharing has proven far more laborious and challenging than anyone had dreamed. As a result of a careful management study, Gill has determined that it will be necessary to employ approximately fourteen colonists in the tasks of interviewing stricken families and accurately assessing their needs. Others will transport the aid to the needy homes, while others will make sure no well-off Animals are hiding or understating the amount of their reserves. Luckily, the greater pig family has exactly fourteen able-bodied beasts seeking employment. For this work, they will be paid from our supplemental gathering: surplus shares of food collected in addition to those for hungry families."

"*Supplemental* gathering?" grumbled Bruce the cow. "That's the first I've heard that term."

"That's the first anyone's heard of it," interjected Norm. "That's why I'm called the town crier. To give you the very first news, before you hear it anywhere else."

"I told you they'd take more," muttered Jevin to his father.

Hoss merely shook his head in resignation and walked on towards the fields.

Before they left earshot, however, they heard Norm's voice proclaim. "And now for our Great Truths. Truth number one: 'He is who is hungry has a right to eat!'"

Hoss' ears pricked up, and Jaxon turned to his father with a questioning look.

"Dad, that didn't sound like, 'Any Animal who refuses to work, should not eat.'"

"It sounded different to me too," Hoss admitted. "The wind must be playing tricks with our ears."

The day's rain was, thankfully, no isolated occurrence. It rained off and on for three straight days, then every week for a month.

The drought was officially over—nearly as quickly as the Colony had found its solution. The rest of the summer was damp and hot, as in a normal year.

Those who, like Hoss, had chosen to heed the first raindrops, saw their corn shoots emerge strong and healthy. In contrast, some of their doom-and-gloom neighbors did not consider planting worth the trouble. Their crops were not mature enough to withstand the summer's heat.

By late spring, the stalks in most of the fields had grown thick and hearty. The naysayers who had stood by wringing their hands, shaking their heads and rolling their eyes at those trudging to the fields, were suddenly nowhere to be seen. Some merely stayed inside, not wishing to face those they had ridiculed. Others, weary of the high temperatures, sneaked off to distant watering holes for hours of cooler amusement.

Another development took place which placed an even greater contrast between the industry and initiative of the harder working beasts and their less-motivated brethren. One of the newly-arrived beaver clan had come to Hoss one night with an idea. While many of the Colonists were seeking respite from the summer heat, Hoss, Champ, his sons and several dozen other enterprising colonists went to work. First, the beavers cleared out a large swath of forest and used the logs to create their largest, most ambitious dam upon a nearby creek. The horses helped them pull the lumber, cutting the construction time by two-thirds.

In return, however, the beavers allowed the other colonists to use their crude plows for a whole new purpose: digging a water diversion channel over to the newly-cleared space. The waterway would now serve to irrigate Champ's and Hoss' largest cultivated field. The result was a triumph of Animal agriculture—a field which received so much regular watering that its yield grew in four times thicker and taller than any other crop they had ever planted.

By the harvest several months later, Champ, Hoss and his co-laborers had more than replaced all that the Sharing had taken from them. Better still, the beavers had received invaluable assistance which had left them with a greatly expanded territory. Territory so vastly increased, in fact, that they even designated a beach at one of their ponds for the Colony's children to splash in, safe from swift and dangerous currents, during the season's hottest months. It was indeed a winning idea for all involved.

In fact, when other farm families came forward to ask if similar irrigation setups could be built for them, the builders saw no reason to hoard the invention for themselves. Instead, in return for a small amount of Wampum or a modest share of future yields, they promptly agreed to help build beaver ponds and diversion trenches for the others, as well.

When Gill heard about this, he and his group of employees whom he now called "colleagues"—a throng which now numbered close to thirty—walked up for an inspection.

Hoss glanced over at the pig. He noticed that the fine hairs which covered Gill's body were now neatly combed, his pink skin shone with cleanliness, and he seemed to have added a good five inches to his girth. He was even sporting a neatly woven neckband of black wool around his neck, twisted in front to form a sort of human-looking tie.

Colony work seemed to agree with the porker.

"That is mighty ingenious," Gill said with a raised eyebrow to Hoss, who stood beside him flinging sweat from his soaked brow.

"It's just another example of what we Animals can do when we're free of human tyranny," Hoss said, his smile of old restored. "In fact, the kernel of the idea came from one of our new beaver friends, over there."

"Well, this will certainly be a boon for the whole Colony," Gill said admiringly.

"What do you mean?" Hoss asked.

"For the Sharing, of course. This extra grain is going to relieve a lot of misery this winter."

"But the Sharing was a temporary measure," Hoss protested. "To get us through *last* winter. That season ended a long time ago, and the drought is over now. We planted this for our own families!"

Gill shot Hoss a look of dismay. "But the deprivation hasn't ended. The gap between rich and poor is still with us. Another winter is on the way, and those in need have no more food reserves than they had last year. You've had the good fortune of stumbling across this revolutionary advancement—you're not honestly planning to keep its blessings from your fellow citizens, are you? 'For our own families'—really, Hoss, you should hear how selfish that sounds."

"I, we..." Hoss corrected himself with a swipe of his long nose towards his fellow farmers standing to one side, "planted this in order to replace what the Sharing had taken away! We were glad to help others through the winter, and now we're glad to replenish our own family's reserves. That's all."

"I'll tell you what," Gill said with the magnanimous look of a leader addressing his flock. "Why don't we vote on it?"

"I have a better idea," snorted Hoss. "Why don't you keep your promises?"


That very night, Gill called a meeting at the Colony's center. Hoss stood first and gave his best explanation of how he and those with more reserves had been pleased to help out during a crisis. After they thought things had improved, however, he and his associates had sought a way to work a little harder and replace what the emergency and the Sharing had cost them all. The result had obviously proven so successful that Hoss even offered to show anyone who asked how to grow such a field for themselves.

No one spoke up. None of the listeners seemed interested in taking Hoss up on his labor-intensive offer.

"I'm sad to see that no one is interested in working for their dinner," Hoss said, "as I and my friends have done. But I'm not surprised. I remember all of those who stood by, shaking their heads, when many of us and I went out to plant a crop before we were sure the drought had ended. I saw how last summer, some were more interested in water sports than in agriculture. I was disappointed to see that no one who received the Sharing used their share to either plant their own new crop, or save some for this coming winter."

Looking deflated, Hoss ended and shuffled over to his spot on the sidelines.

Then Gill took the speaking spot. Before even saying a word, he began slowly shaking his head, as though sadly disappointed by what he had just heard. An expression of fatherly wisdom ruffled across his brow.

"Those canals look dangerous, crossing the fields like that. I fear some non-swimmers could fall into one and drown. My job as leader is to protect our citizens."

The horses exchanged appalled glances when several cheers went up at the suggestion.

"My fellow Colonists," Gill continued in a speaking delivery which had only grown more powerful and forceful over time. "I'm sure that most of you, like me, clearly understood what our dear Hoss, in his advancing years, must have failed to hear. That is, the Sharing was meant to last as long as injustice did. Yes, we had some rain—just enough to replenish the coffers of the well-to-do. But did the emergency end? Do all of you have enough grain and food to last this coming winter?"

"Nooo! Nooo!" shouted back a large portion of the crowd, in an almost musical response.

"Are you all prepared to be thrown back to your own devices to eke out the winter as best you can?"

The *noooos* redoubled in volume and power.

Gill turned to Hoss with the befuddled look of someone who has no choice.

"Our dear Hoss, I was elected to be leader of every Animal in the Colony; not just the wealthy and brilliant. And as long as the Colony's children face the prospect of a winter without food, as long as there are poor and hungry among us, I will stand up for the Great Truths which define our Colony!"

"Which Truths?" asked Hoss.

"The very first, specifically. You should know that, Hoss. 'Every Animal has a right to eat.' You're seeking to deprive us of that most basic and life-giving right."

Hoss's head shot up, his eyes brimming with anger. The Great Truth had been rewritten!

"What about *our* rights?" interjected Gander.

"What rights do you mean?" Gill snapped back just as quickly. "Your right to take food out of hungry children's' mouths?"

"Take food *out*?" Gander replied, disbelieving. "I'm just talking about keeping the fruit of my labors!"

"You sir, are proposing that we suspend the Sharing, effectively snatching the very life-giving nourishment right from the mouths of hungry, malnourished children from your very own Colony!"

A rumble of *boos* took shape and began to grow in volume. Soon, it engulfed the stage and seemed to visibly push Gander backwards, out of speaking range.

"Fellow Colonists, let us take a vote right now. Should we suspend the Sharing and let Hoss and his rich friends keep more spoils than they could ever want or need? Should we suspend the Sharing and thus take life-giving food away from our brothers and sisters and their precious little ones? Should we turn our backs on Great Truth Number One?"

"But there's no 'suspending' to it," argued Hoss. "The Sharing was supposed to end automatically, as soon as the drought was over! Technically, it's already ended!"

"You believe that you have a right to unlimited wealth, but you do not believe a disadvantaged child has a right to dinner?"

"You're putting words in my mouth," Hoss protested. "Words I don't believe!"

"Well, try these words on for size," Gill continued. "The Colony's Health Safety and Environmental Committee has decided that your irrigation system is dangerous to the lives of our colony's non-swimmers. Furthermore, it diverts the natural flow of water from the river. You are hereby ordered to backfill the soil you removed, to its original location."

Before anyone could object, Gill raised his front leg before the crowd.

"Vote, everyone?"

Within seconds, the Colony had voted overwhelmingly, as Norm's town-crier announcement would phrase it the next morning—to *protect the citizenry and the environment, and safeguard the Sharing on behalf of everyone's fair and just right to eat and survive the winter.*

# Chapter Eight

Because of the bountiful harvest, those who had worked made it through the winter. Those who had chosen not to work also made it through, as Gill's associates simply gathered food from those who had worked, and distributed it to them.

Surviving the winter brought with it an air of celebration. The hero of the hour was not, as one might have expected, Hoss and those who had worked so tirelessly. For the recipients of the Sharing, the hands-down hero was Gill, their champion who had bravely stood up for the rights of the poor and disadvantaged.

Gill was the first to articulate, in words they could understand, how the less fortunate were actually victims of the greed and selfishness of those victimizing them. All winter long, town crier Norm grunted long messages from Gill, backed up later by speeches from the Leader himself. Each one alleged the deep-seeded injustice of the Colony's former state—in which Animals were left to fend for themselves. According to Norm, the strong had lorded over the weak and those unfortunate enough to suffer injury or illness had simply been 'out of luck.'

Bruce the cow, whose home had been rebuilt by a joint workforce of Colony volunteers before Gill's rise to

Leadership, tried one cold morning to argue otherwise. He pointed out that his family's misfortune, and that of others, had been quite generously addressed without the need for Sharing. He was promptly shouted down as a crony of Hoss, an exploiter of his cozy relationship with "The Horse."

Before long, Hoss and those who shared in his hard-working habits began to avoid the center of the Colony's compound, especially during Norm's morning speeches. It seemed all their presence earned them were long, angry stares from the other listeners.

Furthermore, Norm's reports were always doom and gloom. If the sky wasn't falling, the economy was in peril. Norm consistently ended with one abiding litany—*we need to expand the Sharing so the environment and the Colony's victims can be protected!*

One winter's day, as leader Gill and his buddies strutted through the colony's Pond Sector, they noticed an emaciated pig shivering in the cold. He lay just outside a neighboring beaver's hut, trying to stay warm by using the hut as a wind block.

Gill reared back in shock at the sight of him and asked in a loud voice, "What is your name and why are you out here? Where is your home?"

"I don't have a home," offered the pig. "They call me Hopeless."

"Why, that's an interesting name. Why did your parents name you that?"

"My original name was Hopeful, but that name didn't stick."

Soon a small crowd had gathered, and Bucky the beaver came out to see what the commotion was about. Upon seeing the fat, furry rodent, Gill frowned and asked him in front of everyone: "How can you sleep at night knowing this poor pig is out here shivering in the cold?"

Bucky replied, "I sleep very well, thank you. Hopeless has been hanging around this neighborhood the entire summer and fall. Several of us have offered to help him build a shelter and gather food during the harvest, but he wasn't interested. I even offered him a job in my construction business, but he only wanted to sleep all day in the shade, then party with his friends all night. He actually laughed at us for working so hard and not enjoying life, as he put it. So we decided that he would have to learn his lessons the hard way."

"That does not change the fact that this poor creature has no shelter and no food to eat," countered Gill.

The next day, Norm reported that Leader Gill had been inspecting the Pond Sector when he had come across an emaciated, starving pig right next to the elaborate home of a wealthy, well-fed beaver.

"Our Leader Gill demanded to know why, in a colony of such wealth, there could be such a contrast."

Norm glared. "I would like you all to meet Hopeless."

A shivering and emaciated Animal limped into view. Norm began humming, then singing full-throated, a song entitled *Everyone Deserves a Home.*

Among the listeners, not a dry eye remained.

The next morning, Norm's news report was emphatic. "Our leader has decided that enough is enough. The wealthy have gotten rich off the backs of Animals like Hopeless for too long. Gill has called for an immediate Sharing hike on the top one-percent of Colony earners. He has also promised that the added grain and Wampum will be used as an entitlement for those, like Hopeless, who have been left behind. In fact, Gill will be proposing two new laws to handle this pervasive problem. The 'Economic Equity and Anti-Poverty Act' will make economic injustice a crime. And the 'Anti-Hate and Equal Employment of Pink Animals Bill' will prevent employers like Bucky from hiring beavers over pigs to cut down trees and build dams."

A week after the laws' passage, Bucky was startled to find a group of dogs outside his door. They were there to collect the retroactive Shares authorized by the Colony, along with a hefty fine. His construction company's payroll did not contain an equal number of 'pink Animals'—pigs.

The following week found the beaver in front of a judge appointed by Gill. The judge ruled that because Bucky could not pay the fines imposed, his home would be confiscated and turned into a Colony-subsidized dwelling for unfortunate Animals like Hopeless.

The bold action only reinforced Gill's reputation as a fighter for the poor and disadvantaged. However, it did little to improve Hopeless' lot. That next spring found the young pig and his friends living in squalor, in a dwelling now ruined by neglect. The neighborhood was by then riddled with trash and abandoned due to its reputation as a gathering place for thieves and vagrants.

Bucky soon moved his construction business beyond Animal Colony's borders, triggering a prosperity loss that grew into a Sector-wide unemployment problem.

By the time the Animals learned of this, it had become Norm's newest outrage story about the cold-hearted nature of the Victimizer Class. His early summer message was that Gill was working on a program to extend unemployment benefits for those who had lost their jobs when Bucky moved. He was also looking for a way to punish other employers who moved any portion of their businesses away from Animal Colony.

A month later, Cotton, the bull who had suffered a severe injury and emerged as one of the heroes of the Freedom Battle, lost his long fight to remain mobile. His lingering wound had, over time, finally robbed his left front leg of all movement. He and his father Bruce had been two of the Colony's hardest-working stalwarts, constant companions to Hoss and Gander in the fields.

To make matters worse, Cotton had just taken a new mate, Emma, and they had a calf on the way. Cotton reluctantly went to his father for help.

After hearing his son's reluctant plea for aid, Bruce hung his head and sighed sadly. "There is nothing I would rather do than help you right now," he said in a mournful whisper. "All I've wanted to do, my whole working life, was to help my children. It's the reason I worked so hard for so long. But there's a problem."

Cotton nudged his father's nose inquiringly. He had never heard his father admit defeat before. This tone of voice was something entirely new to the young bull.

"In past years, there would have been plenty. But since the Sharing, the Supplemental Sharing, the Additional Administrative Sharing and the Surplus Sharing, I have barely enough to feed your mother and our new calf. It's amazing that all this started with just one emergency sharing, and grew into this. It's like one of those runaway tree vines."

The old bull looked down at his son and sadly shook his head. "I am so sorry, son. But I have nothing to give you." Bitter tears gathered in his large eyes. Finally, he could look no more, and glanced away.

"Didn't Gill promise that the Wampum for his new free child care program wouldn't come from working class Animals like us?" Cotton protested. "He promised to actually *lighten* our Sharing load."

"I remember," said Bruce, "and since I'm not wealthy, it sounded good to me. I was all for taking care of children––especially if it didn't cost me anything. But it didn't work out that way. First, many of the rich started to leave, taking jobs with them. Others simply started working less to make sure they weren't considered 'rich.' Some stopped working altogether so they could qualify for Gill's handouts."

The old bull fought back a bitter snort and looked away.

"When I went to buy fresh bedding straw from Champ the other day," Cotton said, "I noticed he had doubled his prices. I asked him why, and he told me he had to raise them to pay the new Sharing and stay in business. I realized that the rich aren't the only ones paying for Gill's programs. We *all* are."

"Yesterday," said Bruce, "Gill announced that since we are in hard times, he now considers anyone with a job to be 'wealthy.' When I heard that, I remembered something I had not heard in a long time: *Great Truth Number Four.* The more we reward Animals for being poor and needy, the more their numbers increase. And when we penalize Animals for being hard working and prosperous, their numbers decrease."

Finally, Bruce sighed heavily and looked his son somberly in the eye.

"Son, I have nothing to give you, but you and your family can come live with us. We'll do what we can to feed everyone."

"But if I move in with you," said Cotton. "I won't qualify for the Sharing myself."

Bruce had no reply.

So, with his heart breaking, Bruce watched his son hobble with head lowered over to the Colony House. This brand new, sprawling building housed all of the Colony's administrative functions, but it was best known as the place where beleaguered Animals signed up for Sharing benefits.

If rumor was true, the new building, whose construction had employed so many Animals, was also Gill's new family home. The pig had let it be known that although he and his family did not favor sprawling dwellings, they would sacrifice for the Colony's sake.

"For you, my friends," he had announced, "I will drag my family into an over-heated building rather than the natural, simple pig quarters our kind prefer. Since my work requires me to be on call at all times, it forces me to live virtually in my office. It is a great strain on my nature-loving family, but no hardship is too great to bear in the service of our beloved Colony."

When Bruce's friends had questioned Gill about its rumored opulence, he had explained the difference between his abode and Champ's by announcing, "Comfort brings me no joy, as it does victimizers like Champ and Hoss. It only helps me remain an even more effective champion for the victims among us. In that mission, I need all the resources possible to carry out this daunting task."

Those listening nodded in silent amazement at the depth of Gill's dedication. Surely, there was nothing this pig would not sacrifice on behalf of his fellow Beasts.

The next morning, Gander rousted his three young goslings, Benjamin, Abby, and Emily, for a day in the swamp learning essential goose feeding techniques. Being typical adolescents, they protested the early wakeup time, quizzing their father on the need for such drastic measures. But Gander refused to even address their sullen questions until they were outside and underway.

"Your mother and I have been far too easy on you so far," he said as they stepped across the Colony compound. "It's high time you pitched in on an adult level to help find food. The two of us simply can't do it alone anymore."

"Why? Are you getting too old?" asked Emily their youngest in an anxious tone.

"No, it's not that—yet," he replied. "It's just that, with the way things are, the harder I work, the more of my harvest gets taken away for the Sharing. Before Gill took over, I was able to work in the field while your mother stayed home to teach your older siblings about life. Now, she also has to work outside the home and we have neglected teaching you how to be good citizens and responsible adults."

Just then they passed the Colony's center, where Norm was crying out the day's news.

"Once again, Leader Gill's efforts to secure equal rights for all Animals are being thwarted at every turn! The efforts of the Hossian elements to channel resources into the hands of their friends and cronies is making it harder to bring our citizens essential rights and services!"

Ben turned to his father. "What's *Hossian elements?*" he asked with a frown.

"I don't know," Gander confessed. "I've never heard the word before."

A bystander turned around and smiled at them indulgently. "It's a new word," he whispered. "It means 'in sympathy with Hoss.' It basically means someone who's selfish and wants to keep as much as he can for himself. Someone who hates those who are less well off, and wants to punish them for their poverty."

Gander nodded and gave his son a helpless shrug. He glanced around at the growing crowd of mostly younger Animals, milling around for a closer listen.

"Why are so many adolescents here?" Gander asked his children. "Is this where you go when I'm away at food-gathering?"

The goslings turned and gave him the kind of looks adolescents are famous for—shocked, disbelieving expressions that make their recipient feel like the most ignorant beast on the planet.

"Duhhh…." said Abby.

"Why aren't they with their families?" Gander asked, almost to himself.

Abby shook her head, as though wearied by the task of explaining everything to a decrepit father.

"Nobody hangs around with their Mom and Pop anymore," she sneered. "Most of my friends don't even live with both their parents. And the parents that stay together are too busy out rooting for food all the time."

"But being part of a strong family is the best way for this community to continue," Gander said, his voice rising in anger. "If nobody works, there'll be no food for the Sharing, and nothing for hard-working Colonists to eat!"

"Dad," said Ben with a roll of his eyes, "the Sharing never runs out."

"Don't count on it," Gander snapped. "Food production is way down these days, because no one wants to work. I used to hire chickens and ducks to pull weeds for me while I spent time with your siblings. Now I have to do it myself.

It won't be long before we will have to bring in Animals from outside Animal Colony to do the manual labor. Unfortunately, that solution will only last until they can qualify for the Sharing. Then, the colony will just have more non-workers to support."

"My friend Taylor the chicken wanted to get a job so she could buy her mom a bowl," Abby said, now starting to pretend she wasn't even walking beside her ignorant father, "but no one would hire her because Gill has told business owners that every Animal must be paid a living wage. The shop owner asked Taylor why he should hire inexperienced adolescents when he could hire an experienced adult for the same wages. She answered, 'So I can get some experience?' to which he simply said, *goodbye*. None of my friends really plan on working anyway. It's easier and more fun to just hang out. Some of my girlfriends say they're trying to have babies so they can qualify for housing and higher Sharing allotments."

"But who do you think pays for the Sharing?" Gander asked, fighting hard to contain his frustration.

The three offspring turned to him and shrugged.

"It's just... *there*," Benjamin replied at last. "It's all the food and wealth the Colony produces. It gets put in one place and shared fairly, among everybody. Not just your grumpy old rich friends, Dad."

Gander rolled his eyes. "Let me explain why I don't agree with Leader Gill. He doesn't trust in liberty or the Creator to keep things in balance. He believes it's his job to take responsibility away from the individual and provide every Animal's needs. He doesn't think we're smart enough to spend our own Wampum. He wants to be everyone's Mom and Dad. For my part, I think the Colony should leave responsibility with the individual and family, more like…"

He pointed to a group of young Animals kicking around a wooden ball.

"… like the referee at one of your hoofball games. Their job is to penalize those who break the rules. They protect the players from fans, like the Colony should protect its borders."

A shout went up as one of the teams scored. Gander counted the players silently, and continued.

"They make sure each team has the same number of players and doesn't form a monopoly, which destroys competition. Likewise, Animal Colony shouldn't let large businesses merge, because monopolies give them the power to treat their customers and employees unfairly.

"But the referees don't tell the players how to play the game. They don't feed and shelter the players. They don't treat injuries. They don't take points from one team and give them to the other to make everything even. It's their job to guarantee equal opportunity, not equal outcome. They make sure there's a level playing field, and that's all. Does that make sense, kids?"

"I guess so," the three said in unison.

With that, Gander motioned with his head for them to leave the area.

"We don't do this nearly often enough," he muttered darkly, almost to himself. "I think I'm learning more than you are."

They walked away just as Norm introduced a brief, in-person appearance by Leader Gill. A raucous cheer went up from the assembled spectators.

"Hoss and his friends try to scare you, telling you that for every bag of grain we gathered for the Sharing, only a half-bag is given back to actual needy citizens. But who do you think works to carry out this redistribution? Does the reserve gather itself?"

"Nooo!!" went the crowd.

"Do the Shares magically distribute themselves around the Colony?"

"Noooo!!!"

"Do these hard-working fellow citizens, laboring night and day to preserve your right to eat and be healthy, do they deserve to be paid? To feed *their* families?"

"Yeahhhh!!!"

"Then it's no mystery where that extra half-bag is going, is it? My fellow Animals, don't let their self-motivated scare tactics frighten you!"

The pig's now-practiced speaking voice rose in volume and pitch, throbbing over their heads.

"I will not let them roll back the rights that have been denied you for so long! This kind of fear-mongering will not stand!"

Another cheer rose up, so powerful that it seemed to physically blow them from the area.

"Dad, can we go back now, and hang out with our friends?" asked Emily.

"Yeah, do we have to go swim around that smelly swamp, pulling out pond scum with our beaks?" added Benjamin.

Gander sighed. "It's what we do, kids. We're geese. We float and we gather water plants. It's how we were made. Would you rather go poking in the dirt for grain some pig throws down in front of you, like a freeloader?"

"Daddy, what's a *freeloader*?" she asked.

He raised his eyes to the heavens, searching for an answer. "Somebody who lives off the labors of others. Kind of like…"

He glanced backwards, then thought better of it. Instead he shook his head and faced the approaching swamp. Reaching the mud at last, breathing the wet smells that once meant everything to him, he shook his head and began to silently wonder if the whole experiment which was Animal Colony truly had a chance to survive.

# Chapter Nine

Several days later, as Hoss and Gander made their way to the Central Delegates' monthly visit with the Colony Leader, they stopped in to see their friend Bruce. One look at the old bull's face was enough to make the two stiffen and stop in mid-greeting. Something was clearly wrong.

"What's the matter?" Hoss asked Bruce, who had motioned for them to come inside.

"I'm worried about you two, actually," Bruce answered with a look of warning. "You're becoming quite unpopular among the Sharing employees. As I have, for that matter."

"Why? I love them all dearly."

"Oh, not according to Gill," said Bruce. "He tells everyone working for the Colony that you're out to take their jobs. Yank the food out of their children's mouths. Did you hear that they're expanding the Sharing load again?"

Hoss shook his head, his eyes brimming over with a sadness the others could hardly bear to see.

Gander shook his head. "I hear there will soon be a Share taken from every transaction we make between ourselves. Plus Shares added on to the price of everything we buy and sell. Even a full half-Share taken out of what we try to leave our children when we die."

"Unbelievable," muttered Bruce. "Pretty soon, nobody will want to produce anything. There's rumors that more of the farmers and business owners are moving away from Animal Colony completely, to places with lower Sharing rates and legal irrigation. "

With that, Gander realized they were due for the Council meeting. They left with a heavy heart.

By the time they reached the meeting spot, a room within one of Animal Colony's new and ever-expanding headquarters, the atmosphere was already tense and charged.

Gill was addressing the other Delegates as they walked up. The Leader was now resplendent in a bright blue, berry-dyed wool tie, knotted with a flourish around what once, in thinner days, would have been his neck. Today, the pig had grown so fat, even for his species, that it seemed the decoration had been intended to create the appearance of a neck where none existed. But that was not all: his bulging wrists, which even now carved the air in grandiose gestures, were marked by stark white folds intended to mimic the very smartest fashions.

"We are in a dire crisis," he was saying in a most cultured and smooth speaking voice. "A few greedy Animals and the lack of government control over our Wampum exchange have caused a financial collapse. Because of the urgency of this crisis, we have already started a bailout to protect the economic interests of every

Animal. Even though revenues are way down at the moment, an additional infusion from our Sharing base will make up the difference…"

"Wait a minute, Gill," Hoss interrupted as he walked in. "Are you saying that you're planning to take even *more* from us?"

"Only from those who can afford it, Hoss. As you know, it's our patriotic duty to *share* our resources with each other."

"Patriotic duty?" bellowed Hoss. "Your Great Readjustment has been a great failure! Today, Animal Colony is far worse off. We're no better equipped to survive the coming winter than we were before the Sharing. You're right; we are in a dangerous situation. And yes, food reserves are down. But the problem isn't the fault of one or two Animals. It's the result of your policies and of your pals who use your policies to their own advantage! You've allowed your business buddies to break our rule against monopolies. You want us to think this bailout of yours will solve the problem? It's actually just an excuse for you to take control of another huge chunk of Animal Colony! Just another example of you trying to look good by pretending to solve a problem you created in the first place!"

"What?" shouted Gill. "Are you now accusing me of being a *thief?*"

"I'm accusing you, sir, and all your friends who caused this crisis," replied Hoss, "of being lousy managers of what you take in!"

Gander raised his wing to speak. Randall the Moderator reluctantly gave him the speaker's stump.

"We are all concerned about the poor and want to help those in need," Gander honked in a soft voice. "Some true victims truly need help, directly from those of us who can. And some true victimizers do need to be punished. There are also true champions of victims, whose goal is to help victims grow into self sufficient *non*-victims."

He fixed the Leader with a piercing gaze.

"Gill, I once gave you the benefit of the doubt. I assumed that you truly wanted to lift everyone up out of their plight. But now I see that you actually feed off those poor beasts who trust you. These dupes believe they're actually the victims of anyone with more than they have. Victimizers, you call them. You may seem and sound like a true champion but in reality, Gill, *you* are the victimizer!"

The great pig gave out a great bellow of outrage mixed with fury. "How dare you make such an accusation!"

"I dare," continued Gander, even more fiercely than before, "because your support base consists of Animals trapped in a cycle of dependence created by your own policies! Think about it, everyone," said Gander as he turned to address the representatives, "his answer to every situation, however minor or temporary, always involves raising Shares and more government control and new programs that never go away even though they don't work. Our history shows that taking Wampum away from our citizens simply makes everyone poorer and more dependent on Gill's help. This in turn increases his voter base. He rewards incompetence and failure, in direct violation of our Great Truth Number Four that *whatever we reward will increase*. This is why it's actually to his *disadvantage* to solve problems!"

That was more than Gill could take. The Leader seemed to forget that the meeting's purpose was for Sector delegates to communicate with him. The great pig turned bright red, belted out a series of ear-splitting screeches and jumped forward, seemingly intent on leaping right on top of Gander.

The whole room filled with an enraged clamor. A group of security dogs immediately ran forward and caught him, restraining his great surge. Despite themselves, Gander and even Hoss backed away, threatened by a whole cordon of enraged Animals.

Gander turned to his old friend. It struck him that in his whole life, he had not seen a sadder look upon the old horse's face.

"Let's go, Gander," Hoss said in a voice so drained of hope and vigor that the goose hardly recognized him.

"So much for letting our voices be heard!" Gander shouted, ironically drowned out by the tumult.

The pair turned around and walked out, surrounded by a group of equally frustrated supporters.

The very next evening, Gander returned from his fieldwork to find several Animals standing outside his shelter, chanting angrily and pumping their feet into the air.

"Down with the politics of fear!" shouted one. "Keep your values out of my wallet!" chanted another. "Families are for fogies!" stayed popular for several loud rounds. They ended with several minutes of "Bullies stay home!"

Gander rushed inside to find his children huddling around their mother with wide-eyed, terrified expressions. They had never witnessed public displays of hostility like this one before.

"Who are those Animals?" asked his wife Gloria, her eyes round and wide.

"Just a bunch of youngsters making nuisances of themselves," he ventured.

"I don't think so," Gloria said nervously. "Gander, I saw Gill watching from a distance in the woods. He was clapping his hooves together and waving. Honey, I think these are Colony employees, doing this on Colony time."

Gander looked out again, a grim look upon his face.

"Gill has finally ruffled my feathers once too often. I think he has just declared outright war. That's it. We need a new Leader!"

# Chapter Ten

That winter's usual hardships were magnified by a marked economic downturn. Its cause? A loss of jobs from employers moving their operations out of Animal Colony, in search of places with friendlier business climates. Business owners could see no end to Gill's hunger for the Wampum they needed to stay in business, make a profit and hire more employees. They found that it was cheaper to make their products somewhere else and then haul them back for sale to Animal Colony citizens. This caused an enormous flow of Wampum away from the Colony, where it could have circulated and nurtured the general prosperity.

As a result, the Colony was poorly prepared for the cold season. It seemed the normal joys of life which had come from strong families and the satisfaction of hard work were disappearing. A malaise seemed to hang over the Colony, interrupted only by angry shouts from those demanding a larger and larger portion of what they considered to be their rightful portion of the common wealth.

Mercifully, spring arrived with a vengeance. Warm temperatures came quickly and powerfully, raising temperatures from below freezing to cool and wet. A cool front blew through and stayed for days, dumping inch after inch of rain upon the entire Colony.

Within days, the harshness of cold and snow had been replaced by the threat of impending flood. On every side, creek levels rose and currents of murky water began to invade the Colony's low-lying areas.

Hoss petitioned the Colony Water Authority to let him make repairs on the series of dams and levees he and the beavers had built several winters before. They were the very ones that had offered the promise of great prosperity to those wanting to irrigate their fields. Perhaps, he reasoned, a few improvements might at least steer any future floodwaters away from the Colony's center.

However, Hoss' request slowed to a crawl as it was routed through government channels for approval. Colony officials had taken over the beavers' masterpieces months before, as part of a public works improvement project. It now lay in ruin, an embarrassing hulk of tangled lumber and stagnant water.

The name on the request did not help, of course. Hoss had indeed undergone a dramatic reversal in the hearts of his fellow Colonists. Through Gill and Norm's tireless public-relations efforts, he had become the number-one enemy of social progress and hope. No longer praised and revered for his role in the Colony's founding, or his bravery at the historic River Crossing or Freedom Battle, he had now become little more than a solitary figure in the forest, quietly applying his strength and size to the hardest tasks.

It did not help that Gill's bureaucracy had decided history was not important. "Thoughts of progress into the future should occupy your minds and time," schoolchildren were told by the Director of Educational Standards, "not vain boastings of the past."

So when it became clear that official approval would not come in time, Hoss took it on himself to perform the repairs, unpaid and unaided. Without consulting anyone else, he recruited a pair of beavers to cut down some timber and began hauling logs night and day, trying to turn the dams and levees into an improvised flood control system.

All too soon, the waters began to rise dangerously, but Hoss only deepened his resolve. Even when the lowlands were flooded up to his haunches, Hoss continued his plodding effort to do what he could.

On the fourth day of heavy rain, disaster struck. Owls came screeching out of the sky, warning of impending danger.

Seconds later, a high, brown wall of water swept across much of the sector by the river—the same area Hoss had asked residents to avoid after the last flood.

The onslaught washed away homes, food and many of its citizens. In two or three moments of rumbling terror, screams filled the sector.

The once-familiar area transformed into a cluttered, bracken lake of death and destruction.

Hoss was working alone, upstream from the Colony in the thickest part of the forest, when he felt the soil shake under his hooves. He strained his ears forward and heard a noise like thunder approach from the northwest.

His brain processed two thoughts, almost in unison.

First, this had to be the flash flood he had been working so hard to prevent.

And second, he was in the worst possible place in which to outlast it.

Hoss turned in the sound's direction. Instead of the tree branches' usual dappling of greens and browns, he saw a wall of milky brown. The dreadful sight was growing nearer, taller, and louder with every passing second. He could see and hear the tide crack and smash through undergrowth and smaller branches. With a tug of dread on his heart, he spotted loose logs, some of the very trunks he and the beavers had labored to cut down, being tossed about like twigs atop its leading edge.

The coming menace suddenly felt to the old horse like some sort of angry beast, on its way to devour him. For a moment, he despaired and wondered if he had the strength to resist it.

Dread paralyzed him for a moment, followed by a surging resolve to save himself. Hoss turned at last and willed his legs to move, to quicken into a faster gallop than he had run in years.

The path ahead was far from clear. The abandoned projects of beavers and bureaucrats alike had left the forest floor strewn with a jumbled mass of fallen timber.

And yet run Hoss did, summoning forth reserves of energy he had feared long dead. With one great leap he launched himself over a fallen log and landed hard, then took off again. Logs and twigs swept past him and dug burning grooves along his flanks. He shook his head at the pain, snorted in denial and quickened his pace.

One thought struck him, through the drumbeat of fear and physical agony. *This feels familiar.* It felt to Hoss like he had been trying to outrun a coming wave of destruction for a very long time. The gathering doom he had sensed for so long now felt as though it had taken physical form and finally launched its attack.

Still galloping his hardest, he strained to see the clearest way ahead. But then, seeing only thicker forest, he glanced behind and realized the raging torrent would not run out of energy. It would not stop until it reached higher ground—and there *was* no higher ground anywhere close.

So what was the use of running?

Frenzied thoughts roared through his mind, one after another. *I can't just surrender*, he told himself. He still had honor and gallantry, values which suddenly felt more real and precious to him than any worldly treasure.

Through all the frenzy came a bitter thought. He'd lingered into an old age which had stolen nearly everything he'd once cherished—like the glow of his old vision for the Colony. Or the admiration of the Animals he had once led. Even his influence over their future.

And after all that, what did this cruel moment leave him to pass on? What kind of heritage would he leave his sons if he lost his honor now? He had always taught them: *Never quit. There is always hope.* Clearly, giving up in this ultimate test would tarnish a lifelong example of courage and risk-taking.

He felt another wave of determination surge through him, alongside the pain and terror. *He would not give up.*

That resolve swept through Hoss just as the waters overtook him. With a helpless floating sensation, he felt his hooves lose contact with the ground and the current sweep him away. His very steps, once proud and resolute, were now under the water's power. Tree trunks sped past on every side. A massive oak rushed towards him, not twenty paces ahead. Although he stretched his limbs and paddled with all his strength to try and avoid a collision, the effort did little to alter his course.

In the final second before impact, Hoss clenched his teeth and flexed every muscle within him. Despite the water's complete control over his destiny, he strained his body into the motion of one last, futile lunge.

*I have fought the fight*, he told himself as the great trunk loomed abruptly before him. *I did not surrender.*


To the survivors' relief, Leader Gill was at his headquarters on high ground when the flood wave swept through.

However, nearly everything near the river was washed from place. Bedraggled and demoralized survivors huddled on the high ground, desperate for safety and aid.

That is when the second disaster struck: the Colony government's attempt to help those in need. The director of public safety was now Bernard the dog, a holdover from the days when defense against attack was of primary concern. But such matters had faded so far from priority that the public safety budget had been reduced to a pittance. As a result, the sector had no plans in place for evacuating stranded Animals to a proper evacuation spot, to say nothing of countless other concerns. The citizens, conditioned by years of speeches, simply concluded that Gill would take care of everything.

As a result, countless survivors, half-alive and dying alike, hung on stubbornly to various trees and branches and waited in vain for rescue. Several of the horses, a species tall enough to withstand deeper water, began wading through and picking up whomever they could.

Hoss, however, could not be found. His sons and their mother could be heard frantically combing the forest, whinnying in vain for their beloved father and mate.

They searched alone.

Most of the Colony's food, now stored in holding areas rather than in individual homes, was now destroyed. Worse yet, distribution of what little remained turned into a catastrophe. The chain of command broke apart as hungry Colony workers began to demand their full share of meals before helping anyone else. Food fights broke out; much of the spare grain was stomped into the mud.

The evening after the flood's first onslaught, Cotton's body was found by beavers, floating some three hundred yards from where his home had stood. The inactivity needed to qualify for Sharing had weakened him so badly that he had grown too frail to resist the flood.

The body of his young, sickly calf was found nearby. It took another day to find the corpse of her mother Emma. She had possessed the strength to reach safety, but had chosen instead to launch into the deepest currents in a desperate bid to save her family.

Gill, the only Animal seen that day dry and well-groomed, walked through the ravaged area dishing out a wealth of encouragement and exhortations. Sighing loudly and shaking his head in a vague lament, he announced that

Hoss' ill-designed and unauthorized tampering with the Colony's state-of-the-art flood control system had obviously caused this tragedy's deadly toll. Nevertheless, he promised, he and the Sharing would work magic with their usual speed to bring food, new shelters and infrastructure.

"As soon as possible," as it turned out, took quite awhile. The Department of Public Safety delivered Wampum to those in the flooded area, but there was nowhere to buy anything. The department delivered tents as temporary shelters, but someone had forgotten to include the poles and stakes necessary for them to actually function as protection from the elements without blowing away.

The floodwaters themselves did not recede from the compound until the beavers at last convinced Gill to let them finish what Hoss had started. Then, with a concerted effort of private citizens—horses, cows, beavers, even dogs—a new, improvised channel led waters away from the area and out into an existing beaver pond which quickly tripled in size.

Only then, when the ground was exposed to light and air again, did the full cost of the disaster fully reveal itself.

Inside their shelters, countless numbers of the Colony's citizens were found dead and rotting on the earth beside all their strewn possessions.

At last Hoss was found, lying unconscious and barely alive, on a beaver dam not far from where the floodwaters had first swept in. He was pulled by a mournful team of friends to the one place he would have least wanted to be the Colony's official health care facility.

# Chapter Eleven

The medical building was built of sticks, mud and birch bark like the other buildings of Animal Colony, but it had been white-washed inside and out with lime to make it seem more clean and sterile. Outside there snaked a long line of Animals waiting to be seen. Some stood, while others lay down, too weak or injured to remain upright. Many bled from areas where their bodies had been rammed into trees or rocks while being swept along by the flood.

Hoss' friends and family pleaded that his injuries were more severe than most. They were rebuffed, reminded that Colony policy called for everyone to wait their turn.

So he waited.

After about an hour, the duck in front of them turned around "You can move ahead of me," he said. "I have a kink in my neck, but they'll probably just give me some willow-bark to cover up the pain, anyway. What I need is to have the bone in my neck put back in place, but the Colony won't pay for manual adjustments. When the flood hit my shelter, one of the beams came down and hit me in the head and I felt my neck pop and here I am."

Hessie whinnied softly. "It's kind of you to let us go ahead."

"I recognized Mr. Hoss,' the duck continued. "He is hard to miss. Besides, I don't believe what Norm is telling everyone. All this destruction can't be the fault of Hoss just tampering with the flood protection system."

"Good for you," Hessie said in a low whisper. "Don't believe anything you're told."

"Not anymore," the duck continued with a shake of the head. "I believed Leader Gill when he promised that his new and improved healthcare system would solve all the old way's inequalities, as he called them. But I live right across from this clinic, and I've seen nothing but long lines ever since Gill took over the system. From what I see, his equal care has translated into equally *poor* care."

Hoss' family shook their heads sadly at the duck's words, then resumed their long wait.

When they finally dragged Hoss to the entrance hours later, they saw a corridor lined with rows of Animals lying on piles of straw.

The receptionist, a meek ewe with braided wool framing her face, said, "Patient's name please?"

Hessie said, "Mr. Hoss, and he needs to see the doctor right away. He's unconscious and has lost a lot of blood."

"The nurse will see him as soon as we find some more bedding."

"Nurse?" asked Hessie. "Where is the *doctor*?"

"His shift ended hours ago. But we do have a nurse, and I can assure you, she is very good."

"You mean you have only one nurse," asked Hessie, "to take care of all these Animals—and no doctor?"

"Well, the staff, including the doctor, can only work their regular shifts unless special permission for overtime is granted by the Department of Health. For all we know, the administrator got washed away in the flood. He did have a resort home down by the river, and he hasn't been seen. Meanwhile, we have to follow the rules. Besides, a directive came down two weeks ago to cut staff and not waste expensive procedures on the elderly. How old is your mate, anyway?"

Hessie responded. "It is none of your business. Can Dr. Barnaby be called in? I'm sure he would be willing to help. He always seemed to know what to do."

The receptionist shook her head emphatically. "Mr. Barnaby is a natural health care practitioner, and the natural types are not allowed to practice in the Colony's clinics. As I said, the nurse will be with you shortly. Please wait along with everyone else."

Hoss regained consciousness inside the clinic, greeted by the loving faces of his sons Jaxon and Jevin. Both horses, laced with superficial cuts and bruises, stared down at him with grateful looks.

"What happened? How is the Colony?" Hoss asked in a barely audible voice. "I was far away and alone when it struck."

"Well, the River Sector flooded again, dear," Hessie said hesitantly. "Thanks to all your hard work, the water didn't reach as high as the last time. Still, there's been great destruction and loss of life. You've been badly hurt. You're bleeding from your head and from your left side."

Hoss shut his eyes with a pained look. "I should have tried harder. I should have started asking sooner. I should have taken my case to the citizens."

"It's not your fault," Jevin broke in. "The citizens know you're a hero, and that you tried your hardest to stop it. At least, the citizens who matter, anyway."

"Did Gander make it?"

Hessie nodded with a smile. "Gander is a goose, remember? A waterfowl. His kind fared the best of all."

"Could you please bring him to me?" he asked.

Several minutes later, Gander stepped to his side. Hoss asked for some privacy, motioning for his friend to lower his head so they could speak privately and he would not have to shout.

"This may be our last chance to turn Animal Colony around," Hoss muttered between labored breaths. "If ever these Animals are going to be disenchanted enough to listen, it should be after Gill's failed promises to keep them safe. But I am not the one to lead this fight. I want you to call for a vote of the whole Colony on ending Gill's Readjustment once and for all. Gander, I truly believe now is time for you to run for Leader. We may not get another opportunity."

"I don't think he'll even allow a vote."

"Then gather every sympathetic and disgruntled citizen you can," Hoss muttered, fighting for every syllable. "Remind them about the time disaster struck and the government actually stayed out of the way. Remind them how Animals used to volunteer their homes. How we pulled together and repaired the damage without government help. March on Gill's office if you have to. He has no argument to stand on. He's always said the Animals' wish was his command. Debate him, right before a vote is taken. That way you can say your peace without Norm putting his spin on it. Then the Colony can make an informed decision."

Gander nodded thoughtfully. "A chance to talk. That, I think Gill would go for."

They both laughed softly. But just then, Gander saw blood trickle from the corner of Hoss' mouth and a slight gurgling sound when he took in a breath.

"Help," Gander cried, "Hoss needs help! Where is the doctor?"

"Oh, as I told your friends, he went home hours ago", replied the nurse, "and we are now closing the clinic. I'm sorry, but your friend will have to wait till morning."

"But he can't wait that long," begged Gander. "He won't survive without your care!"

"Again, I'm sorry, but the clinic closes when the clinic closes. The staff is ready to go home. And you must too. The rules are the rules!"

Hoss received no further care.

Late that night, lying alone on a pile of straw in the clinic hallway, Hoss took his last, labored breath and died.

His family returned the very next morning at sunrise and waited for the clinic to open. Just as the door finally swung open, Gander flew up, breathless.

"So sorry I'm late," he said, out of breath. "I had a few delegates to speak to this morning."

The group walked to the front desk nurse as one.

"I am here to see my husband," Hessie asked in a subdued voice.

The nurse looked down darkly, then took a deep breath and looked Hessie straight in the eye.

"I'm sorry to tell you this. Mr. Hoss expired early this morning."

"What?" asked Jaxon in a strangled voice. "He died?"

"Despite our very best efforts, I'm afraid that yes, that's what it means," the nurse replied.

A horrible pause descended on the group. The two sons whimpered softly. Hessie stood utterly still for a long moment, her only outward sign of emotion, a pair of tears swelling at the bottom of her large brown eyes.

"Can we see him?" asked Hessie,

"I'm sorry," came the reply. "For viewing, you'll have to go to the Director of Environmental Impact and await further instructions."

Upon arriving at the administration building, they were met by a stern faced sow who hurriedly asked the nature of their business.

"We're here for permission to remove my husband's remains from the clinic, hold a memorial service… and then bury him," Hessie said, her words quivering with emotion.

"I'm sorry, but we are unable to release the remains to you at this time." she said with a defiant turn of her snout. "However, you can make the release go faster if you pay the fees up front."

"All right," said Hessie, her features clouded by grief. "What'll it be?"

"Let me see here?" Ten pieces of Wampum for return of remains and seven for the internment tax. Oh, and are you planning to bury or cremate the remains?"

"We planned on a traditional burial."

"Oh. Then for an Animal of his size, there will have to be an environmental impact study. That's quite a costly undertaking—no pun intended. Consultants, engineers, Animals digging around, you know. Of course, if you are a Share recipient all this will be paid for you. I don't suppose you are a Share recipient?"

"No, I am not," answered Hessie with an icy tone. "I am a Share *contributor.*"

"Then, you might want to reconsider."

"Reconsider what?" asked Hessie who was getting more and more frustrated.

"Reconsider burying or cremating his remains."

"What do you mean? Is there an alternative?"

"You could donate his remains to science. You know, so doctors can learn more about the Animal body and use that knowledge to help others with health problems."

"Will his body be treated with respect?" asked Hessie.

"Of course. After the healthcare professionals gather the knowledge they seek, the remains will be disposed of in a dignified fashion in accordance with department policy."

"Well, Hoss was always a giver," she said wistfully, glancing first to one son, then the other. "He dedicated his whole life to service. I imagine he would also want his death to mean something. What do you boys think about giving his body to science?"

Both agreed that this is what Hoss would have wanted.

They would hold a memorial service in two days, and invite his family and friends.

Two days later, the mourners gathered at Freedom Rock for Hoss' body-free memorial service. It seemed fitting that chilly autumn winds had chosen that very day to sweep through the forest, sapping the warmth from any Animal who dared venture outside.

As a result, only a meager and shivering group gathered around Hoss' fresh marker. The large memorial of driftwood had been foraged by his devastated beaver friends and laid beside Freedom Rock, the place of his greatest triumph.

Hessie and his sons stood up front, their long faces still clouded by grief. None watching could tell whether their shivering was due to weeping, the cold, or both.

Gander stepped forward to speak. Before he could, a rustle swept through the group and Leader Gill walked up, arrayed in a black tie. His sagging face was now a mask of solemn respect and mourning.

"May I say a few words?" Gill asked in a restrained voice, and no one thought of denying him. "As someone who helped me start this Colony, I can honestly say that

Hoss was once a friend of mine. You might not think so for all the disagreements we endured later on, but it's true. From those early days, I cherished Hoss' courage and incredible sense of fairness, even if those qualities later failed him."

The great pig seemed to change topics with a deep breath and a preening turn of his flapping neck.

"And, as the one in charge, I am so relieved to learn that the Colony clinics gave him such attentive care during his tragic final moments. Today, I only ask that we remember Hoss for the good things he gave us, not his harmful beliefs or legendary stubbornness. For the good sides of his character, and those early days when he displayed them most clearly, I want to say thank you."

Gill smiled blandly, seemingly aglow in the warmth of his mercy and generosity. He nodded once at Hessie and walked away in silence. Hoss' friends watched him leave with barely audible sighs of relief.

"It's up to us now," came Gander's voice at last. "Hoss is no longer here to inspire us with his wisdom and his amazing work ethic. If his vision stands any chance of surviving, then it is through this group right here. We cannot lose heart, or turn away from the challenge ahead. Hoss would not want it."

Just then a gust of harsh wind raced down from a grim, grey sky, chilling their faces. Gander shivered violently and paused for a moment.

"Friends, let us leave Hoss' beloved wife and sons alone to say good-bye in their own way," he said in a voice cracking with emotion.

Without another word, the Animals most loyal to Hoss——Gander and his family, his horse relatives, beavers, Barnaby the Owl and a scattering of geese—turned and filed away from the river with the forlorn gait common to such occasions.

As Gander and his family left, he sighed heavily, sounding like one who had just been stripped of life's greatest joy.

"There should have been a national day of mourning," he told Ben in a sullen whisper. "The whole Colony should have been here to pay respects."

After a long walk along the old path that had now grown into an established forest trail, they rounded the Colony center. Here lay the very spot Hoss had gazed upon, on that first dawn, and proclaimed his vision fulfilled—the Colony's home after an eternity of anxious trekking through virgin forest.

Gander looked away, up into the sky and its black-tipped clouds.

"It's coming," he mumbled.

"*What* is coming?" asked his wife.

But Gander did not answer, his eyes filled with anguish. He only shook his head.

An hour later, the rain clouds blew away and left a clear blue, warm fall sky. Norm the town crier emerged, and for once had a standing-room only crowd in attendance.

"Fellow citizens, I have the honor of presenting Gill, the esteemed Leader of our Colony."

Met by strong, if not enthusiastic applause, Gill stepped forward. "My brothers and sisters, I have some news. While attempting an act of vandalism against Colony property, our first Leader Hoss suffered a grave injury from which, despite the heroic efforts of our clinic medical experts, he did not recover. Even though he was a proponent of activities and positions harmful to our Colony, Hoss nevertheless played an important part in its early history. Our prayers go out to his family and friends."

Gill then paused, as though forming the prayers at that very moment. Then he coughed loudly and continued.

"The occasion of this awful flood has brought with it a chance for reflection and hope as we work together to form an even more just and fair society. We see it in the new homes being planned, in the faces of young survivors about to return to school, in the plans of my colleagues thinking ahead for a new and improved Animal Colony. As part of this opportunity, we are going to hold a vote on my policies and plans for a prosperous and progressive year ahead. In addition, Mister Gander has apparently mustered the necessary support in Council to force a vote on certain issues. Namely, whether we should continue the Great Readjustment or make him Leader and go back to the earlier policies of the Hoss Administration. So as we clean up and work hard to build a better Colony, give some thought to the choices ahead of you. And I look forward to seeing you at a debate between me, your leader, and Gander, the goose, on the eve of Election Day."

# Chapter Twelve

Two days before the pivotal vote, Gander's son Benjamin returned from school with a troubled look on his usually energetic and happy face.

"Dad, are you really going to fight with Leader Gill tomorrow afternoon?"

The goose laughed and shook his head. "No, of course not. Where did you hear something like that?"

"All the kids at school are talking about it. They say you and Leader Gill are going to duke it out tomorrow and that probably, blood will spill."

Gander chuckled again.

"You know that I'm running for Leader because I believe if Animal Colony can return to the values that made it great, its best days are still ahead. So tomorrow, Gill and I are having what's called a debate. That's where I'll stand up and tell everyone why they should vote for me, then he stands up and does the same."

"So whose blood is going to be spilled?"

"Nobody's, son. Nobody's blood will be spilled."

"Oh."

There was a long pause.

"Daddy, was our Escape from the Humans motivated by greed?"

"What? Greed?" Gander wasn't sure he even liked hearing his son use the word. "Of course not. Who would have suggested such a thing?"

"Well, my teacher for starters. Not to mention the whole student body. They're teaching history now, and they said we abandoned the Settlers in their time of need, motivated by greed and something called *lust for power*."

Gander fought back an urge to scream and moved closer to his son. "What else did they tell you, Ben?"

"They said bad things about you, Daddy. And especially Uncle Hoss. About the Attack. My teacher said you were something called a war-monger who almost got everyone killed."

Gander's eyes flew wide open, his anger so palpable that even Ben stepped back in fear. "What is your teacher's name?"

"Darvy, the pig, Daddy. But don't worry. I didn't believe her. She said that the real hero of the attack was Gill."

"Gill was there, but he hid in the bushes!"

"No he didn't, Daddy. He actually—"

"Son, I was there. I saw what happened. Gill cowered in a mulberry bush. And Hoss charged the enemy lines with a complete disregard for his own safety."

"Teacher also told me that no one is free as long as one person has more wealth than anybody else. And that you were asking the Colony to take away everybody's rights. Are you doing that, Dad?"

Even though he was nearly shaking with anger, Gander kept control long enough to gently rub the back of his son's head. "Have I ever tried to take away your rights, Ben?"

"Well, I don't know, Dad. She also said the family is an instrument of domination by the strong over the weak. I think I understand what that means."

"But do you agree with her?"

The gosling thought for a long moment, then slowly shook his head.

"No, I don't, Dad. I don't feel dominated. Mostly, I feel loved, and taken care of."

Gander's eyes suddenly glistened.

"I'm so glad to hear that," he muttered shakily. "Thank you. And when it comes to all this talk about the Colony and what it should do, just remember the Four Great Truths I once taught you."

"I never forgot, Dad," he said proudly. "I still remember them word for word!"

Then the young one's face fell. "It is too bad about the Creator, though."

"What about the Creator?" his father asked.

"That he doesn't exist. And that if he ever did, he didn't create us. That was the first thing they taught us."

The day of the great debate arrived, cool and clear. After the trauma of the flood and its messy aftermath, the event became an occasion for the entire Colony to come together. Not only did the Animals anticipate the spectacle of a historic debate, but also the chance to simply gather and celebrate.

Animals began to gather early in the afternoon to claim the best viewing spots. They were greeted by a site that resembled a summer fair more than a somber political event. Volunteers had gathered trash, trimmed leaves and erected colorful wool banners, dyed with bright berry juice. Two special podiums, carved from tree stumps, marked the spot where both of the height-challenged speakers would make their cases.

For a moment, as all the species mingled together in the sun, Gander felt a pang of nostalgia. His mind returned to previous feasts, back in the Colony's earlier and more carefree days. The memory was a wistful and even bittersweet one, since the Colony of today hardly resembled the carefree yet hard-working version of yesteryear.

Many of those assembled could not remember eating a meal not handed them by the government.

Finally, in late afternoon, Norm stepped to his usual town-crier position.

"Friends and fellow Colonists," he began, "I face you today not as the crier of daily news, but as a celebrity host of the debate we've all been waiting for. Let's be candid: we have not faced such a stark choice since our historic escape from the human settlement. We were then faced with the decision of whether to stay or to go, to brave the freezing river waters, or turn back."

The older listeners nodded knowingly.

"Today, we face two equally clear options. Shall we elect Gander as our next leader and return to the policies of yesteryear? Or shall we stay with current leader Gill and continue the progress and fairness of the Great Sharing?"

Gander turned to the host with an incredulous look, aghast at the blatant bias of Norm's words. Opting to remain silent and let the outrage pass, he settled for a glowering shake of his head.

"Here is our great Leader Gill, with his opening statement."

"Thank you Norm," Gill said four times in a row, waiting for the roar of cheers and applause to settle.

Almost a minute later, the adulation had not died down, so he continued anyway.

"My friends, I face you today in the fight of my life—or, should I say, the fight of *our* lives. I come with a thrilling plan to finally achieve Animal Colony's promise of true equality once and for all. Mister Gander, however, wants exactly the opposite. He wants to roll things back years into the past. He would actually turn back the clock and strip away even the few essentials I and our Colony brethren have fought so hard to win for you. Everything you now have, all the victories we now celebrate, would all be smashed and thrown away."

A resounding storm of boos and growls filled the speaking area, so deafening that it made Gill lean backwards as though bracing a stiff wind. But rather than recoil against it, Gill strained forward again.

"Will we let our lifeblood get sucked away by the victimizers of our bitter past?"

"NOOOOO!!" bellowed his supporters.

"If you will re-elect me and turn away from the politics of exclusion and elitism, I will not only send them a-packing, but bring my innovative plans into action to move us forward. My friends, the rights to food, shelter and health care for all, were only the beginning. After that will come free educations, as high as your children want to pursue them! We will take your children and teach them all they need to know to become worthy citizens in our new social order! You may ask how we are going to pay for this new program. We are going to simply raise the Sharing amounts on those who can afford it—the wealthy. My plan will actually lower the Sharing amounts on all of you in the middle class!"

Forgetting that Gill had made the same promise before and failed to deliver, the Animals unleashed an immediate and emphatic roar of approval. Clearly, a huge segment of this crowd believed that Gill would consider them "middle class" and loved the idea of paying less in Sharing. Wild applause ensued with shouts of, *Gill! Gill!*

"Candidate Gander," offered Norm. "Would you like to make your opening statement?"

Immediately, the volume died down to a hostile hush. Gander turned to face a sea of glaring faces. He searched for a moment to find those friendly to him, and finally located his own family and a few friends and supporters in the third row. Smiling gratefully at them, he cleared his throat.

"Thank you, Norm. I also want to thank all of you for coming today. My dear friends and fellow citizens, each of us stands here because only a few years ago, our founder Hoss, the Father of our Colony, received from our Creator the dream of a place where we could live as free Animals."

Gander paused and looked out over the crowd. If any of the hostile watchers had a clue what he was talking about, they weren't giving a hint.

"Allow me to start by describing what this dream *was not*," Gander continued. "It wasn't what we see today. Not even close. It wasn't a colony that promises you everything in life handed to you as a present. It wasn't a colony that takes away ever-increasing amounts of a family's hard-earned prosperity, then lets half of it rot before tossing it over to other Animals who didn't work for it. It wasn't a promise to let the government rule every part of our society. It was simply—*liberty*. Liberty is a complicated word, but it basically means letting us do what we choose, as freely as we can without trampling on anybody else. Only in liberty can we work, achieve and produce to our fullest. Only in liberty can we be everything we were created to be. And that's what I propose to bring back, my friends. A return to liberty. The opportunity to thrive in freedom."

Gander stepped aside, his final word immediately drowned out in a chorus of angry shouts. Small objects began to fly his way through the air. A rock struck his leg, then a strip of moss flew past and curled around his beak.

The goose glanced down at what, for his species, was actually food. "Thank you for the snack!" he called out with a faint grin.

"Mister Gander," yelled Norm, "may I remind you that your time is up! You are to refrain from making statements until your turn has resumed!"

"But—"

"You lose a turn! I'm warning you, Mister Gander…"

The goose turned to his family and shrugged with a perplexed look.

To break the silence, Norm called out, "Leader Gill, what is your rebuttal? Please take two turns to answer."

"Thank you, Norm. My beloved fellow creatures," Gill began, "Instead of the past, let's talk about change. And hope. My opponent wants you to believe we've already given too much, tried too hard, to ensure a better tomorrow. Ever fearful of new ideas, he asks you to throw up your hands and say no, enough of this. Enough of hope."

Boos now rose openly from the front rows. Not against Gill's actual position, but his mocking version of Gander's.

"Oh yes—enough of hope, Gander will tell you. Enough of dreaming that someday equality and opportunity will come to every single member of Animal Colony, and not only to the fortunate. Instead, let's return to the hunger and despair and deprivation of yesteryear. Let's call that liberty, and hope everyone forgets how imperfect, how... *stressful*... yesteryear actually was. I know. Because I was there."

With a flip of his curly tail and an impish smile, Gill ended his introduction. The crowd gave him a delirious ovation. They chanted, *Hope for the future! Hope for the future!*

"Now it is time for the question and answer segment," Norm announced. "First question for Mr. Gander."

A middle-aged duck stepped to the front and cleared his throat.

"Mister Gander, what is the most important difference between you, and what you offer, and Leader Gill?"

Gander looked up and down, trying to phrase his reply. Finally, he looked the questioner straight in the eyes.

"Let me answer with a question. Do you remember seeing how humans used to tame a wild Animal? First, they would lock it up in a pen where it could no longer forage and feed itself the way the Creator intended. Then, they would show up every day with a ration of barn-barrel food and feed it to him, straight out of their hand. Before long, the poor beast forgot how he ever provided for himself. He came to believe there was only one source for food: the human Master. The Animal then woke up in the morning and walked over to where the Master would show up with his ration, and waited. He had become a slave. And so have many of you. Gill is slowly enslaving you by making you forget how material blessings came from the fruit of your own labors, not a handout from his bureaucracy. If you choose to work, Gill takes so much of what you create that you become less able to provide for your family. It's his hand on the bridle, his way of forcing you into servitude. Soon, you've heard his twisted words for so long that you forget you ever had freedom, that you were ever able to provide for yourself. Instead, you crave and cheer for the half-rotten foods he gives you from his own hand, as if they grew out of his personal kindness. Friends, we did not venture into the unknown wilderness and escape tyranny, only to walk right back into a tyranny of our own making!"

Norm put up his hoof, stopping Gander. He turned to Gill and brightened with a sunny smile, extending a gesture towards him.

Gill stepped up, his broad smile now gone. "I will not waste your time trying to correct all the mean-spirited accusations spun by my opponent. His Sharing-cut scheme, and his talk of freedom, are all about the freedom to keep what others need. It is all about helping his rich friends hoard more of the Wampum and provisions they made off the backs of you who worked for them. His friends want to keep their Wampum so they can more easily control all of Animal Colony. It is Gander who wants to enslave *you*!"

Gill stepped back as the crowd seemed to erupt into not only jeers and boos, but a wave of snarling and growling. The once controlled audience now seemed perilously close to violence. Gander looked down, trying to decide whether to stay or not, and was aghast to see the security dogs pulling away, letting down their protective barrier.

He was being visibly threatened.

"Am I allowed a rebuttal?" Gander called out.

Norm cut his eyes over at Gill, who nodded ever so slightly. Norm turned back and waved his hoof. "Be our guest, Mr. Gander."

"Gill has accused me," Gander began, "of not caring about the poor, the sick and the disabled. He accuses the working Animals of only being concerned about ourselves and our Wampum. But don't you all remember how before the Sharing, families took care of themselves yet also had the resources to help others? During crises we all pitched in and helped rebuild. We were like one large caring family, even as we treasured our self reliance. We did not look to our leader and our government to take care of all our needs."

Gander paused and looked around, appearing to ponder whether he should speak his next words.

"Some of you remember how my father, Samuel, traded his leg for his previous freedom. He endured the excruciating pain of cutting off his own leg with a piece of flint. Freedom is worth sacrifice. Here is that very flint."

With that, Gander flipped the grayish stone out into the crowd. Silence fell as everyone stepped back in the form of a rough circle and stared at the sharp edged stone.

Many of the young could not remember its significance and were unimpressed. While the crowd continued to fix their gaze, Gill trotted out, came down with his hoof, and ground the object into the mud.

"Your flint means freedom for you and your friends to take advantage of the weak!" howled Gill. "To the rest of us, it means freedom to fail!"

"That's not true!" broke in Gander, barely audible above the cheers that accompanied Gill's previous comments. "I just want us to return to the Great Truths which brought us so much happiness and prosperity. They have all been changed, sabotaged to create the hatred and class warfare we see today!"

"I was there when the Great Truths were adopted," countered Gill. "They were never meant to be rigid, fixed statements. They were intended to be beautiful living words that could change and grow as Animal Colony moved forward into a fairer future!"

Gander turned to the crowd and nodded forcefully. "The Truths, son!" he shouted. "The Truths!"

Suddenly, a young goose voice rang out high and clear above the crowd. It was Ben, Gander's son, reciting through a choke-hold of fear and intimidation.

"Number one: *he who refuses to work, should not eat*!"

"Silence!" shrieked Norm, now red-faced and slinging spittle in his rage. "Only appointed debaters can speak!"

"I yield my time to my son, then!" cried Gander.

"And he is misquoting the Great Truths! A crime against the Colony! You forfeit the debate!" Norm growled.

"Number two," cried out Ben unyielding, "*Every Animal deserves an equal opportunity*!"

"Outcome!" cried out Gill. "Every Animal deserves an equal *outcome*!"

Ben looked at his Chief Executive with a shock and surprise of a young one discovering adult frailty for the first time. "But Leader Gill, I memorized it just the way…"

"Get it right, you little fool!" Gill snapped.

"Dogs, arrest him!" Norm cried out, pointing at the youngster. "He is willfully desecrating our Great Truths!"

"*The harvest belongs to those who toil for it!*" Ben cried out again.

In unison, a dozen protesters chanted back their own, memorized version. "*Belongs to all those who hunger!*"

At that moment, all remaining illusion of order fell apart. The dogs edged closer to the young gosling, and Gander saw all he could tolerate. As a loving father, he could take no more. He launched himself over the crowd to his son's side and engulfed him under his strong right wing.

Thankfully, Hoss' two sons had also shoved their way to his side. The horses now swept back the surging pro-Gill rioters with heaving lunges of their great necks.

"Let's go, Ben," Gander said sadly, shaking his head. "They're already enslaved, and they don't want to hear about it."

With that, the pro-Hoss contingent of Animal Colony filed out from the debate grounds, audibly chased out by a hurricane of growls and shouted curses.

As they walked away, they heard Norm grunt as he stepped up to the speaker's stump. "Make sure all of you show up tomorrow for the referendum. It is a vital time for all of us who really care about Animal Colony, its citizens and the environment!"

"Don't worry, Pop," Ben was overheard as saying while they filed into the darkness, "You were able to speak your mind. The truth was heard."

Just a few strides away, they saw a crowd gathered around the battered feeding trough which snaked around the *Colony Right to Eat Center*.

As they walked, they glanced towards the crowd milling around the trough. No one even noticed them at first. Instead, the beasts continued jostling with loud grunts and shoves over a smear of gruel and grain trickling from holes in the walls.

"This is the way it was back at the settlers' compound," Gander told his children in a near-whisper. "Fighting with each other over meager handouts. I'd better leave before my other leg is crippled, breaking up another fight."

Ben nodded, remembering the old story of the two roosters fighting over a single kernel of corn.

They turned back again towards the pathetic scene, then headed for home.

As they passed a smaller, fenced-off building, they heard a sudden growling of dogs from beyond the barrier. It was not an angry sound, but that of hounds about to feast.

"Here you go, officers," came a pig's voice. "Just as promised. Fresh horse meat, courtesy of Leader Gill. And plenty of it, this time!"

The words sent a shudder of revulsion churning across Gander's insides. A sickening thought hurled into the back of his mind—one so disturbing that he didn't want to even entertain it.

It couldn't be... They wouldn't do *that*...

*Would they?*

Gander hurried past with his son beside him, grimacing at the sound of slobbering jaws tearing into wet flesh.

He shook long and violently, suddenly filled with the sense that he was somewhere else, someplace utterly foreign and unrecognizable.

He shivered again and realized that the air had grown sharp and biting. Suddenly, he heard a noise which sent another wave of dread and recognition through his body.

It was the sound of a shutter being slammed shut against a fierce wind.

He turned and saw the Colony House, the sprawling building he had never entered because no one but Gill and his fellow pigs were ever allowed inside. A pig's foot had just poked out from a window and pulled its shutter tight. Warm, inviting firelight shone through the last window before the same foot emphatically closed its shutter with another clatter. As always, the sound gave him a shiver.

For a government building, it certainly resembled a cozy home, Gander remarked, glancing up at the greasy smoke pouring from its chimney. Public service had most definitely been kind to Gill and his friends, especially on a night like this.

Gander stopped and shut his eyes against the irony of it all. He remembered that very first evening back at the settlers' compound—that historic night of Hoss' announcement. A wave of melancholy blew through him, more bitter and chilling than the wind's bite.

"Why are you stopping?" asked the gosling.

"Because this is an exact repeat of that fateful evening, son," he said. "A sunset like this, and an icy wind threatening a cold winter. I remember that very sound. The thud of a thick wooden shutter, slamming shut for the winter to keep the Masters warm. The harshness of that sound is what launched us out into the cold night, in search of our own home and a chance to survive the winter."

"You look so sad," Ben said.

"It's because we've come full circle," answered his father. "I feel the same cold knot in my stomach I felt that night. I'm glad Hoss isn't here to see how we threw away his dream."

"Maybe it's not totally dead," Ben said hopefully. "Toward the end of the debate, I saw some of Gill's supporters stop glaring at you. It looked like they were quietly thinking about what you said. Maybe starting to see through Gill's fancy talk."

Gander stopped and gave him a faint smile. "If that's true, then we have one hope left."

"What's that, Dad?"

"Tomorrow, we *vote*."

# About the Authors

**DR. THOMAS A. REXROTH** has been a philanthropist and practicing chiropractic physician for over thirty-eight years. He has a driving interest in causes and solutions. His interest in health, politics and social problems has led to several published articles in national journals. He previously authored *Red or Blue: Which View is Best for You?,* a book describing how conservatives and liberals categorize people and see the world. He has special insight in understanding what made America great and what we must do to help her remain the greatest country the world has ever seen. He lives in Iowa with his wife Sharon, who writes children's books, and is the father of three children and grandfather to nine.

**MARK ANDREW OLSEN** is a screenwriter, author of four solo novels and four collaborative novels including the bestselling biblical thriller *Hadassah,* adapted into the FoxFaith film *One Night with the King.* He co-wrote the MGM film *Music Within,* and the Bethany House novels *Hadassah Covenant, Rescued, The Assignment, The Watchers, The Warriors, The Long Road Home* and *Ulterior Motives.* Mark is the son of Baptist ministers and missionaries to France and a graduate of Baylor University in Professional Writing. He lives in Colorado with his wife Connie and three children.

To buy more copies, please visit animalcolonybook.com.